NICOLA RATNETT

THE GOOD, THE BAD
AND THE STRANGE

First published United Kingdom 2020

ISBN 9798613164585

Dedicated to the team at the Prison Phoenix
Trust for their valuable work

INDEX

A RUM DO

I tapped on the front door, pushed it open a crack and yelled: 'Auntie. It's Mandy.'

'Come in,' a creaky voice answered. 'I'm in the sitting room.'

I walked through the hall – dodging a disgustingly large pile of cat excrement on the new rug – and discovered the elderly lady slumped on the sofa, television blaring as yet another episode of, *"Murder She Wrote"*, played out.

'Hi,' I said. 'How are you today?'

'Angry,' she snapped. 'That bloody man next door has put up a new fence – on *my* land!' She banged the arm of the sofa, dislodged a full ashtray which slipped to the carpet, scattering ash and dog ends.

I squatted on my heels and used an old envelope to scoop up the mess.

'He's a thief, a liar and a pervert,' Auntie grumbled, 'and moves in next to *me.*'

I chuckled and agreed with everything she said. Her new neighbour was a very odd character and a definite fantasist, claimed to be ex SAS and a test pilot for the RAF – amongst other things. Auntie wasn't wrong about the land either, the man had moved his fence at least eighteen inches into her garden.

'I've been on to the council,' she said, 'who don't want to know, and the police say boundary disputes aren't anything to do with them.'

She pulled a cigarette out of the packet and lit it with trembling hands. The first lungful of smoke set off an inevitable coughing fit and I fetched a glass of water from the kitchen.

'Thank you, dear.' She slurped and spilt drops on the woolly blanket which covered her legs. 'The police said I should talk to a solicitor – but why *should* I?' She thumped the sofa again and again the ashtray slipped to the floor. I placed it on a small table. 'Why *should* I spend my savings to recover my own property?'

'One of your cats has had an accident in the hall,' I said, anxious to change the subject. 'I'll go and clear up and make a pot of tea shall I?'

'That would be kind, thank you. You know where everything is.'

I went to the kitchen, put the kettle on and dragged out cleaning supplies from under the sink. While I was scraping up the smelly puddle – trying not to gag – a ginger cat crept in through the open front door. I hissed at the animal and it left quicker than it came in. I carried the tea to the living room and sat opposite my neighbour on a wooden settle.

Auntie sat hunched, like a half-filled sack of potatoes, hair white and unruly, body swathed in fleeces and blankets, the ever present cigarette dangled from nicotine stained fingers. She'd worked as a primary school teacher before retirement and prior to that she was a member of the women's auxiliary air force during the war, helping to man – or woman – the listening stations in Kent. Auntie had good stories to tell when she could be

3

bothered.

Her sitting room was dominated by a large television which she sat in front of all day, every day and loved anything to do with crime; real or fictional. The furniture was a hotchpotch of chairs and bookcases, a coffee table piled with junk mail dominated the centre of the room; the mantle covered with birthday cards – she'd just celebrated her 91st birthday – and an old sepia photograph in a silver frame was tucked between. I'd looked at the photo many times; three young men, little more than boys, wearing army uniform, flat hats way too wide for them. I knew the boy in the centre was Alfred, Auntie's first and only love. She'd told me they had been planning to marry, but he was sent to France and didn't return. His death had broken her heart, she said, and she'd never married.

'I've heard from the hospital,' Auntie said. 'It's cancer in my lung and they say they can't treat me. *Won't* more like, obviously hoping I'll die before they have to spend any of their money.'

'I'm not sure that's right,' I said, trying to placate her. 'The treatment would probably make you very ill.'

'I should have it!' She whacked the sofa again and spooked the ginger cat which had crept in when I wasn't looking. 'Just because I'm old doesn't mean I shouldn't be treated like everyone else. I've paid taxes all my life – I'm *entitled*.'

I changed the subject again. Auntie could be very forceful when she got worked up.

'You said you wanted me to help you burn some papers?'

'Yes, I do. Private stuff, bank statements and bills. We can use the incinerator in the back garden. There's a bagful under the sink in the kitchen and some more in the back porch.'

I was pulling bags from the cupboard when Auntie tottered into the room with her wheeled walker. She perched on the plastic seat and peered at me.

'That cupboard could do with a sort out,' she huffed.

'I'll have a go while I'm down here if you like.' I dragged handfuls of junk into the light and discovered empty bleach bottles, ancient tins of polish, moth-eaten dusters and surprisingly, an unopened bottle of NAAFI rum, circa 1940.

'Wow, look what I've found.' I held up the bottle and Auntie's face spilt in a huge smile.

'I didn't know I still had that.' She took the bottle and wiped dust from the glass. 'Alfred gave me this, the night he went to France. Don't know why – he knew I wasn't a drinker.'

I chuckled: 'It'll be like rocket fuel now, pure alcohol. Might be worth a bit too, maybe your nephew could sell it for you on eBay.'

I gathered up bags of paperwork, carried them out to the incinerator and added the bags from the back porch to the pile. Auntie trundled slowly through the back door and perched on her wheelie seat to keep an eye on proceedings.

'Can you move the bin away from the house?' she asked. 'Put it next to idiot's fence. If we're going to make smoke I want it to blow in his garden, not through my windows.'

5

I scrumpled paper, lit a couple of pages and gradually fed the fire in the bottom of the bin. Before long flames roared impressively out of the top, but the blaze didn't generate much smoke. There was a huge pile to burn and as the flames really took hold, Auntie shuffled back six feet before settling down again, face rosy from the heat. I used a garden fork to break up the burning wads and sparks zipped about the garden like diurnal fireflies.

'Why don't we burn his fence down?' Auntie muttered.

'What?' I stared at her.

'The nutter's new fence. We could burn it down, soak the bottom with Alfie's rum and . . . whoosh. We'll say it was an accident.'

I laughed: 'I'm not sure we can do that. Arson is pretty serious.'

'And who would know? The nutter's out and like I said, it was an accident. We'll pour the rum on the fence and drop a handful of sparks on it. Should burn a treat.'

'What happens if someone sees us or works out what we've done?'

'What if they do?' Auntie snapped. 'I've only got a couple of months left so they can't do anything to me. I'll willingly take the blame – won't involve you at all. You need to let me do this, dear.'

Her eyes sparkled with excitement and the light from the flames. With an agility I wouldn't have thought she had, she heaved herself upright, pushed the walker close to the fence, broke the seal on the rum and liberally sprinkled the spirit on the cardboard thin wooden panel.

6

Before I could stop her, she lifted a stack of burning paper out of the incinerator with the fork and dumped the lot on the expanding puddle.

Blue flames immediately danced on the surface of the alcohol, followed by orange as the flimsy wood caught. Disturbingly quickly the first section ignited and the fire galloped greedily along the entire length. Auntie threw back her head and laughed as I'd never heard her laugh before. The experience was both horrifying and invigorating in equal measures.

'You need to move away,' I told her. 'Let me help you.'

We retreated to the porch and watched, fascinated as the fence was engulfed.

'I'm going to ring the fire brigade,' I said. 'This is getting out of control.'

'Good idea,' Auntie said. 'Make sure you tell them it was an accident.' She caught her breath and began a coughing fit. Seemingly without thinking, she raised Alfie's NAAFI rum bottle to her lips and drained the last half inch. A smile blossomed on her face and she giggled, a sound I'd *definitely* not heard during our long association.

The emergency services were prompt. They quickly assessed the blaze; two firemen dragged a thick hose to the back of the house and quenched the fire, while at least four others crowded into Auntie's small kitchen to fuss over her sweetly and drink tea. We were asked how the fire started and we truthfully said some ashes from the bin had fallen on the fence. We were warned to be more careful next time, then the hose was rolled away, the fire fighters climbed back on the tender and pulled out of the street. As soon as they were gone Auntie laughed long and hard, if only they knew I thought.

A week later the old lady was found by her nephew slumped on the sofa, having slipped away sometime during the early morning. After the undertakers had left he called in and we shared tea and memories of his auntie.

The arson was weighing heavily on me, I don't know why. I knew no one would find out unless I told them, but thought Sam should know about the incredible event – how happy his aunt had been. The longer he was in my kitchen, the more I needed to tell him so eventually blurted out my dreadful secret. He stared at me, eyes wide and full of smile.

'I know.' He chuckled. 'She told me. Don't worry, she didn't tell anyone else and I won't say anything. The nutter next door was apoplectic when he saw the remains of his fence, said some very nasty things about Auntie until I threatened to smack him if he didn't shut up.'

I sighed with relief: 'I'm so glad you know. You should have seen her, Sam, I didn't know she could laugh like that. Fancy her still having that bottle of Alfie's rum, ideal fuel, although after she swigged the last drop, I have a feeling she wished she'd drunk it. Poor old Alfie, getting killed all those years ago.'

'Alfie? Killed? No, Mandy, you've got that wrong.'

'Auntie told me how he'd given her the rum the night he went off to France and how he never came home. She said they were going to marry.'

8

Sam shook his head: 'Such a sad story, she kept it close to her chest and invented the France story as a cover.'

'What? Was there even an Alfie?'

'Oh yes, Alfie was real, the wedding day was planned too, but he wasn't killed in France. He left the old girl standing at the altar in her wedding dress and walked away. No wonder she was so melancholy all her life.'

'Not last week though,' I said. 'Last week she was euphoric.'

BEST OF BOTH

They're rowing downstairs again, proper going at it and it's all my fault. Mum has called Dad a bastard more than once and he called her a stupid bitch. They're loud too, I bet Mrs Thomas next door can hear them. They've been at it on and off for days now, and I'm glad. Why should *they* be happy when I'm so bloody *miserable*? The row started on Monday when Dad confiscated my mobile at breakfast.

'Dan! You know phones are banned at the table.' He lunged and snatched it.

'Give it back!' I yelled. 'It's mine!'

'Sit down!' He slipped the phone in his pocket. 'You will *not* behave like this, you're not a savage.'

'No, but *you* are, taxing my stuff.'

Mum tried to make peace: 'Calm down, both of you. Let's eat breakfast nicely.'

I pushed soggy cornflakes around the bowl, chinking the spoon on the rim.

Ting-ting. Ting-ting. Ting- . . .

'Dan, cut it out,' Dad snapped. 'What's the matter with you today?'

'What's the matter with *you?*' I shot back.

I saw his right hand twitch and for a second thought he was going to whack me. If he did that I'd definitely leave home. They're lucky I'm still here the way they treat

10

me, all their stupid rules that stop me doing what I want.

'I think he should see a child psychologist,' Dad said, as though I wasn't there. 'This behaviour is never normal.'

'He'll settle down.' Mum stroked my hand. 'Eleven is such a difficult age, hormones running riot. You remember what that was like, surely?'

'Yes I do and it wasn't *anything* like this.' He glared at me. 'Sort yourself out, boy, or there will be trouble.' He pushed himself away from the table.

'I want my phone,' I whined.

'You can have it back tonight. A day without won't do you any harm.'

'I *need* it.'

He ignored me and headed towards the door.

'You don't know what it's like,' I said. 'I'm not like you.'

'Damn right you're not! You need to buck your ideas up or you'll be in for a shock when you get out in the real world.'

'I know I'm a mistake and you don't know what it's like.'

'You're not a mistake,' Mum said, surprised. 'You were *very* wanted.'

'You don't get it do you?' I shouted. 'I'm God's mistake, I'm not even really a boy.'

I don't know why I said that, but could tell it hit home. You should have seen the looks on their faces and no one said anything for a long time, they just stared at me.

Dad broke the silence. 'Of *course* you're a boy, Dan, what a ridiculous thing to say.'

11

He stormed out and went to work and Mum drove me to school as though nothing had happened. We didn't talk much in the car and what I said hasn't really been mentioned since, well not to me.

They row about it every night and tonight has been the worst. They aren't even trying to be quiet and I can hear every word. Dad says I'm eleven and can't possibly know about these things and Mum – who I suspect always wanted a girl to dress up and go shopping with – says we should, "explore the issues", whatever that means.

I notice it's gone quiet downstairs and jump when they knock on my door. They don't wait for an answer, but barge straight in. Dad stands by the door and Mum sits on the bed. He looks angry, but she smiles at me.

'Dan, love, we want to talk to you about what you said on Monday, about you wanting to be a girl.'

'I didn't say I *wanted* to be a girl, I said I *wasn't* a boy. That proves you don't listen to me.'

'Don't be bloody ridiculous,' Dad snapped.

'Steve,' Mum warned, 'back off. If Dan feels this way, we should discuss it, at least let me take him to the doctor. We need advice, he could be transgender.'

'Transgender!' Dad spat the word. 'This is a wind-up, Helen. We shouldn't be giving it airtime.'

'No, it's not!' I shouted. 'You're just not interested, you never bloody are if it involves me.'

Mum glared at Dad: 'If you can't be constructive, Steve, it's best you let me and Dan work this out together.'

He slouched out and Mum took my hand.

'Now, love, tell me what's been going on with you and

why you feel the way you do – if you know.'

She looked at me like she really cared, was really interested in me for once and it felt good. She was taking me seriously; noticing me for the first time in ages and I knew I couldn't stop my game. If I told her the truth now, everything would go back to the way it was – no – *worse* than the way it was.

I tried hard to remember what I'd heard about transgenderness, if that was the word.

'Well, I've always known I was different,' I began hesitantly. Mum nodded encouragingly, letting me talk and proper listening.

'I never liked my body and I've always been bullied. The other kids know I'm not right.'

'You've never told us you were bullied.'

'Didn't want to worry you,' I mumbled.

Mum kissed my forehead and told me to carry on.

I made up all sorts of things, all of which sounded like the truth – even to me. I told her that I'd always liked dressing up, especially in actual dresses and that sometimes I'd used her make-up, when her and Dad were out and the babysitter was snogging her fella.

'Samantha brings a boy here?' Mum was horrified.

I nodded. I knew Sam would get the boot, but didn't like her and Mum finding out that bit was true would make her believe the rest.

We talked for ages before going downstairs to talk to Dad. You should have seen his face when Mum told him we were going to call me Danielle from now on and we'd be shopping for new clothes.

13

Everything seems to be going much better now, it's incredible how my life has changed and I get lots more time with Mum when she takes me to the doctor for regular check-ups and counselling. We usually go for a burger afterwards and then shopping. She loves buying me dresses and I'll be honest, I like wearing them. I thought I'd get awful shit at school, but if anything it's been easier. I *did* get bullied before – my ears stick out – but since I've been wearing girl's uniform, no one's said a thing. I know that's because they've been told not to, but I have *more* friends now than I did before.

The girls hang around because they want to teach me how to use make-up, how to do my hair and how to wear my new uniform. Some of the boys just want to know what it's like to be me and I invent stuff they seem to fall for. Even the teachers don't ignore me anymore and one of them is always asking if I'm OK. There's this one girl who I think is a lesbian, she flirts with me every chance she gets and it's getting *really* confusing. She's amazing to look at and could have any of the boys, but seems to want me for some reason and I'm only a boy in a dress.

I don't have to do games anymore as no one can work out which changing room I should use, so I get to stay in the library while all the other suckers go cross country running in the rain. I'm even allowed to use the disabled toilet.

Things at home between Mum and Dad aren't so good, they don't talk to each other unless they have to. Dad's angry all the time and more or less ignores me, but then he did before so not much has changed. It's different with Mum though and one proper parent out of two isn't

14

bad. There has even been talk of Mum giving up work to, 'help Danielle through her transition', whatever that means. Dad wasn't impressed and left home for a couple of days, but moved back when he ran out of pants. Mum grouched about rats always leaving ships first. I'm not entirely sure what she meant, but Dad didn't like it. He started staying late at work and I only ever saw him at the weekends, but even *he* stopped bullying me.

The only downside was endless appointments in doctor's offices all over the place, but I got used to it, usually just a load of talking stuff. A small price to pay for my new life.

Today me and Mum are going away. She's booked us in at a posh hotel in Devon and I've been looking forward to the trip for ages. We're going to a special clinic for people like me. Dad wouldn't come. Mum did ask him but he said he could think of a thousand other things he'd rather do, so we left him behind.

The weather's great, warm and sunny and I'm wearing a new pink sundress. I haven't had my hair cut for ages now, I can feel it tickling my shoulders and Mum bought me some strappy sandals to go with the dress. She told me during the drive that she *is* giving up her job so she can support me through my, 'transition'. All that meant to me was that she'd be home all the time and that was great. She also told me that when we went home Dad wouldn't be there.

'We're having a bit of a break from each other,' she explained. 'He's been working hard lately and is going to stay with one of his mates.'

'Will he come back?'

'I expect so,' she mumbled.

She put the radio on and tuned it to Radio One, even though I know she hates the music and was only pretending to enjoy it. I turned it up really loud and she didn't complain; I could feel the speakers vibrating in the car door. We got to Devon early, put our stuff in the hotel room and went for a wander around the town window shopping, then a meal in an expensive pizza place.

No one was looking at me, no one staring, but then no one knows me here and I do look just like a girl. It's good to be able to blend in. The waitress even referred to me as Mum's, 'daughter' and I wanted to laugh. I've got everyone fooled.

Back in the hotel room, Mum sat me on the bed and said very seriously: 'We need to have a talk about what's going to happen tomorrow.'

'Why? Isn't it another counselling session?'

'Not quite,' she said. 'We're seeing Dr McEwan. He's a specialist in hormone treatment and is going to talk about giving you some medicine, pills probably.'

'Pills? Am I sick then?' By now I knew the things to say.

'No, love, of course not! The pills will be hormone blockers to stop you going through puberty. We've talked about this before haven't we?'

I nodded.

'Later on you'll be given different medication to help your body change shape, you'll start to grow breasts like a girl would, help you look more feminine and begin the process of changing you into a proper girl. Are you still

16

OK with that?' She peered anxiously into my face, ''cos if you're not, that's fine. I can cancel the appointment and we can go home. Whatever's best for you, you know that don't you, Danielle?'

I nodded again, but my brain was working overtime. It was great to get away with Mum for a holiday, but now it was crunch time. I wasn't sure I wanted to take pills. Wearing a dress was one thing, but pills were another. If I became a girl I guessed I'd have to shag boys and that would be *gross*. Maybe I could find a lesbian to go out with – that wouldn't be too bad – but would I have to tell her I used to be a boy? One thing was certain, I couldn't ask Mum any of this stuff and there was no way I could come clean, not after all this time. Dad would be furious and Mum would be hurt, I know she would, and she's been brilliant, fighting for me, treating me special. I didn't want to lose all that.

I thought about it all night, didn't get much sleep and didn't find any answers.

When we arrived at the clinic there was a girl waiting with her mum and instantly the adults started talking. I looked at the girl. She was few years older than me and had an amazing pair of tits. Her short hair was really dark, almost black and she wore a pair of black framed glasses. She looked a bit like Clark Kent from the Superman movies and I fancied her like mad. She was the most beautiful girl I'd ever seen.

'I'm Danielle,' I said, trying to be friendly and offering my hand.

She ignored it and made annoying popping noises

17

with her chewing gum.

'Why are you here?' I asked.

She glared at me like I was a bloody idiot: 'Why d'you think?' she snapped. 'I'm here to get fixed, isn't that why you're here?'

'Do you want to be a boy?'

'No.' She rolled her eyes. 'I'm non-binary. I'm here to talk about having these off.' She squeezed her tits.

Non-binary was a new one on me and I wanted to ask her about it, but didn't want to look stupid so fell back on a childish: 'Why?'

'Because,' she said huffily, 'I want to look like you, like a boy in a dress and these,' she touched her tits again, 'make me look like a girl.'

'So they aren't going to change you into a boy?'

'No way, that's not happening. Non-binary means you aren't stuck in one sex or another, you can choose what you want to be. Girl one day, boy the next, or sexless. It's the way to go.'

She was called into the office before I could ask anything else and I thought about what she'd said. I hadn't realised I could be *both*, maybe I should have taken more notice of what was said in the counselling sessions. Being both had endless possibilities and meant I might not need pills or any nasty operations – that had always worried me.

Coming here had been a good thing because I knew now I could keep the game going without all the medical stuff. I also knew Mum would still support me, she'd put so much effort in over the last months I knew she wouldn't give up now and she had lots of new friends in

18

the 'transgender community'. And; if I could be a boy sometimes, maybe Dad would come home.

I grinned. I could play the game forever and my parents would never catch me out. Nothing will ever be my fault and I'll never be wrong, but I'll always be special. I really can have it all.

BY A THREAD

I love my job. I'm a 'Finder', I hunt down things people want – whatever they want. I work with Bill, facilitator and boss, the person the rich and famous go to with their shopping lists. Clients are always rich and have more than enough money to buy anything they want. It's the *kind* of things they want that necessitates specialist help sourcing them. They make a list, agree a price with Bill, pay a hefty deposit, then he contacts me.

I've never been asked for anything I've been unable to find. Some clients covet works of art, usually items bought at auction by other wealthy, anonymous individuals, who tuck their treasures away in underground vaults. Since teaming up with Bill, I've discovered that everything can be bought; absolutely everything has a price and if a client is prepared to pay *anything,* they can buy – *anything.*

I don't limit contracts to inanimate objects; I'm sometimes asked to find people and once a multi-billionaire ordered a pair of breeding leopards. I travel widely to fill shopping lists and have more air miles than I know what to do with.

I'm working today. A straightforward if risky assignment; I know what I'm looking for and it shouldn't be too difficult to find. I've hired a car – under a false name of course – and I'm in Mid-Wales. The weather is perfect, warm and sunny, roads quiet. I'm crisscrossing numerous back lanes that link isolated hamlets and villages and I see everything. Nothing stays hidden from me when I'm hunting. I stop for lunch in a tiny pub, the public bar probably smaller than my living room. I chat about nothing with the landlord, usual topics, the weather, a smattering of current affairs, but nothing personal, nothing about me. I am utterly generic and instantly forgettable – just the way I like it.

Back in the car I check the map and drive on. Twenty minutes later I pass a small settlement crouching on an expanse of wild mountain land. In the distance – away from the houses – I spot a young child peddling along the verge on a red trike. As I draw closer I see it's a boy, white-blond, dressed in bright, but grubby clothes, probably under three. I flick my eyes in all directions, but there's no one with him; not a soul anywhere.

I slow down and check my mirrors. None of the dwellings front the lane, but edge a cul-de-sac. I wind down the window and slow to a crawl, stopping ten feet in front of the toddler. I watch as he peddles alongside the car and peers up at me. He makes a grunting sound. I smile and say hello. I wonder where his parents are.

'Ride in car?' he asks, stepping off the trike and coming closer. I open the door and he climbs in. This job is turning out to be a breeze. I reach across, pull the door shut, fasten the seat-belt across his small body and drive away.

He doesn't complain and I *know* I haven't been seen, but leave the system of lanes as soon as possible, seeking anonymity on the A-roads and motorways. I tune the radio to a local station and listen for reports of traffic snarl-ups or news of the boy's disappearance, it would be good to know when word got out.

I crossed the Severn Bridge into England and called Bill on a disposable phone. He picked up immediately.

'Charlotte. Everything OK?'

'Fine. On my way back. Where shall we meet?'

'Usual place. ETA?' he asked.

'Hour and a half.' I hung up and concentrated on the drive, watching the boy out of the corner of my eye.

He's picking a thread on his sleeve, his whole attention focused on the unravelling length of red wool. He's not a particularly pretty child. He has beautiful blonde hair, blue eyes and is the right age, but his features are a touch lopsided. His nose is snotty, not quite in the middle of his face and one of his ears sticks out further than the other. His chin is dimpled, forehead high and he looks a bit like a baby hobbit. I hand him a training cup filled with juice and he guzzles loudly, purple liquid running down his chin, some of it puddling in the dimple.

I pull up outside the safe house in Bath and carry the toddler inside, shutting the door with my knee. Bill is waiting for me in the kitchen, a fresh pot of coffee on the table and a playpen in the corner. I dump the boy behind the plastic bars and drop exhaustedly into a chair. Bill hauls his bulk upright, shuffles over to the child and peers at him critically.

He huffs: 'Is this the best you could do, Charlotte?'

'What's wrong? I've satisfied the criteria – age, colouring . . .'

'Yes, you have, but he's not very pretty. In fact, I think he's pretty ugly.' He sniggered at his lame joke. 'His face is covered in snot, you sure there isn't something wrong with him?'

'For God's sake, Bill, we don't print a catalogue! And having a doctor in attendance to check a kid over is impossible. It's not like taking an AA man when you shop for second-hand cars.'

'Not sure the client is going to be overjoyed.'

The boy sensed disharmony and began a whimper that escalated into a wail.

'Mix up some juice and sedative,' Bill ordered. 'As soon as he's asleep we'll clean him up and take some pictures. Hopefully he'll look better with his eyes shut.'

The child nodded off, I washed his face and changed him into a new set of clothes. Brushing his hair, I noticed how fine it was, like doll's hair. I posed him in the playpen, cuddled in soft, clean cushions and Bill made busy with the camera while I sat at the table drinking coffee.

Switching on the laptop, I surfed the net for reports of a missing child in Mid-Wales, but found nothing. He'd been gone over three hours. Someone should have missed him by now. Nothing on local radio either.

Bill elbowed me out of the way laying claim to the keyboard. He uploaded four of the best photos and sent them to the client via the heavily encrypted dark web.

'Now we have to wait,' he said.

Ten minutes went by before an answer pinged in.

'Not suitable.'

Bill slammed the laptop shut angrily: 'Shit!'

'What happens now?' I asked. I'd never collected anything that had been rejected. 'Can we force the client to take him? Breach of contract or something?'

'Like we even had a bloody contract! You've been in this game long enough to know how it works.'

'I've never picked up a kid before and I only did this time because you talked me into it, *'But they're such a lovely couple. Their son died and they can't have any more. Any child of theirs will have a wonderful life, want for nothing.'*

'That and the money!' Bill snapped. 'Don't tell me the money didn't play a part. Why else would a woman steal another woman's child?'

'So what are we going to do with him?' I grumbled.

'I don't bloody know.'

'Can't we negotiate? Come to an agreement? Offer a discount?'

Bill laughed: 'You know as well as I do we can't negotiate with these people. We'll have to get rid of this one and try again.'

I ran my hands through my hair and felt the stirrings of a headache tapping the inside my skull. The silence was uncomfortable.

'I'm not doing it again,' I mumbled.

'You don't have a choice. We took the deposit and although we can't enforce our end of the contract, rest assured the people who placed the order can – and will.'

I wandered over to the playpen and stared at the sleeping boy.

'When you say, 'get rid of him', what do you mean?'

'I don't care what you do with him, but he can't stay

24

here. Put him in the car; lose him somewhere; find another and get back here sharpish.'

'Bloody hell, Bill, it's not like going to the supermarket for spuds.'

'Put a sock in it, Charlotte, like I said, you don't have a choice.'

'I'll want paying twice . . . in advance.'

'Not a chance!' he yelled. 'Get in the car and come back here with a replacement – yesterday.'

Bill was right, I didn't have a choice. I lifted the kid out of the playpen, changed him back into his own clothes and carried him out. I'd settled him on the back seat and started the car before realising I didn't have a plan. I always have a plan when I'm working and not to have one now was disturbing. I headed blindly towards the motorway, turned on the radio and listened to the news in horror:

'Little Joshua Salmon was taken earlier today from outside his home.'

That wasn't true, I thought, he was miles away from the houses.

'A month away from his third birthday, he has blonde hair, blue eyes and was riding his trike when he was snatched.'

Hardly "snatched", I humphed, he'd asked to get in the car.

'A local resident saw a silver car pull up alongside Joshua and the driver – thought to be a woman – dragged him in before speeding off.'

Some of that was right, but who the hell saw me? I was *so* careful.

I ignored the M4 slip road and headed north towards Gloucester, too many cameras and cops on the motorways. I'd be happier changing the car, but that would be difficult with a comatose child in tow. How the *hell* had I got myself into this terrible mess? By allowing Bill to promise me riches – it wasn't difficult to work out.

I drove carefully, keeping an eye open for police and sticking strictly to the speed limit. It would be mental to be stopped by a traffic cop. I glanced at the speedo and noticed I was low on fuel. Bugger! I'd have to stop at the next garage. I checked the kid in the mirror. He was beginning to stir and snuffled loudly, trying to breathe through his runny nose. I'd have to give him some more muppet-juice when I stopped.

Another ten miles and a petrol station loomed ahead just in time, the fuel light was blinking insistently. I pulled in gratefully and pumped diesel, filling the tank to the brim, I didn't know how far I would have to drive before I could dump the boy. Grabbing my bag I went to pay. Getting back in the car, I was horrified to see the back seat was empty.

I scanned the forecourt verging on panic, but couldn't see him. How had the brat got out of the car? Oh God – I didn't lock it! I rested my head on the steering wheel trying to force my brain to work. Another look around, still no sign of him and I couldn't sit here any longer, I was attracting attention. I turned the key and drew slowly away from the pumps, peering round every corner.

My brain suddenly flipped on; if he's gone, he's gone – now *you* should go. I put my foot firmly on the

26

accelerator and headed for the exit. I glanced right, checking the traffic flow, pulled out, cut the corner, felt the tyres kiss the kerb and headed back to Bath. Maybe I'd hunt again tomorrow. All I wanted to do now was take a hot shower and go to bed. Today had been tough.

I parked the car outside the house and peered at the front wheel, looking for damage which would cost me my deposit, but all I saw was a long thread of red wool snagged on the bumper.

FLOTSAM AND JETSAM

We visit the beach regularly, me and my mates. It's become a sort of club house, this tiny cove on the east coast. We light a driftwood fire, drink beer, smoke weed and chat bollocks. Sometimes we fish when the tide's in, but don't take it seriously enough to actually catch anything and thought we'd be friends forever.

We'd met at school. Adam and Charlie are brothers, barely a year between them and thick as thieves. Ben is a year younger and has bright ginger hair. He was bullied mercilessly for it when we were young and had attached himself to our crew for protection; very much a follower, unlike the brothers. They had a reputation, weren't to be messed with and were handy with their fists. We'd all left school a couple of years ago, failed utterly to find jobs or anything useful to do, so spent most of our time together doing what lads do – mischief usually.

It's cold, the warmth of summer slipped away a week or so ago and we huddle close to the flames. The air is heavy with the smell of salt and rotting seaweed, breeze chilly. Adam throws pebbles into the embers, sparks fly and when the moon floats out from behind the clouds, he and Charlie go down to the water's edge to hurl rocks into the waves. Ben and I stay by the warmth of the fire. I'd drunk one too many cans of beer and felt wobbly, the spliffs hadn't helped much, but it didn't matter, I didn't have anywhere to be; none of us did. The nights we shared on the beach were the highlights of our monotonous lives.

'Hey, lads, come see,' Adam shouted from the tideline. 'There's something washing in.'

Ben and me struggled to our feet and shuffled through soft sand.

Adam pointed out to sea. 'Look there, can you see it?'

We peered into the darkness.

'What are we looking at?' I asked.

'Sort of a crate – there – off to the right.'

'I see it,' Ben said. 'What do you reckon it is?'

'No idea, could be anything.'

Charlie stripped down to his boxers and ploughed into the inky water.

'Shit, it's bloody cold,' he yelped. 'Hope it's something worth having.'

We watched him swim towards the dark shape, difficult to see in the blackness of the night. He reached the bale and splashed around it, looking for something to grab onto.

'Bloody hell!' he shouted. 'There's a kid, hanging onto the ropes.'

'Yeah, of *course* there is,' Adam huffed. 'Always the wind-up merchant, my brother.'

'No really! Someone give me a hand,' Charlie yelled. 'I can't do this on my own.'

'Ben, get your kit off and go help Chaz,' Adam ordered. 'Be useful for once.'

Ben reluctantly removed his clothes and waded slowly into the sea, unwilling to take the plunge.

'Get on with it, you pussy,' Adam hollered.

The pair struggled to tow the bale to shore and I wondered if I should help, it was obvious Adam wouldn't. He was like a general, dishing out orders he wasn't prepared to carry out himself. Eventually they floated closer in and we waded out to drag the lump onto dry land, away from the reach of the waves.

We struggled with the bindings and the boy groaned. I had to uncurl each of his fingers from the coarse rope.

'Get him over to the fire,' I said. 'His skin feels like ice.'

Ben scooped him up and headed towards the burning driftwood. We followed, the bale temporarily forgotten.

The boy was small, probably no more than ten, clothes ragged and soaked, hands red and sore, covered in blisters from clinging to the ropes. He coughed, brought up about a pint of sea water, and then vomited on the sand.

'That's disgusting,' Adam grouched, 'Bloody disgusting.'

He wandered away from the fire and down to the sea.

'What's your name?' I asked the boy.

He stared at me, but didn't speak.

I pointed to my chest: 'I'm Dave.' I pointed to his chest and asked, 'you?'

'Amraz,' he mumbled before puking up more seawater.

He was shivering violently, teeth maintaining a constant percussion. I stripped off his tattered jumper, removed my own hoodie, slipped it over his head and tucked it around his skinny body. Ben handed him an open can of beer and the boy gulped the fizzy liquid, setting off another coughing bout.

Charlie thought it was hilarious. 'Priceless,' he laughed. 'A puking Paki.'

I glared at him, spilled the remaining beer on the sand, took the empty can to a stream that ran onto the beach and filled it with water. The boy slurped greedily and his cough gradually subsided.

'Where have you come from, Amraz?' I asked.

He gabbled excitedly in a foreign language.

'Speakee English?' Charlie asked loudly, peering into his face, poking him hard on the forehead with a nicotine stained finger.

The boy stared blankly at him and held his hands out towards the flames, desperate to soak up the heat. Ben discovered a squishy Mars bar in his pocket, ripped open the plastic and handed it over. The lad stuffed it in his mouth and licked the wrapper clean. I went for more water and when I returned the boy was sketching a shape in the sand. It looked like a boat. He mimed the boat capsizing and having to swim, thin brown arms whirling through the air.

Adam returned to the fire, a huge grin splitting his face.

'You'll *never* guess what's in the bundle,' he said, dropping a packet close to the fire. 'It's stuffed full of weed! There must be a hundred plus of those,' he nudged the parcel with his foot. 'We've struck lucky, boys, a hundred kilos of weed and it's all ours.'

'What are we going to do with *that*?' Charlie asked, pointing at the shivering boy.

'It's just a bloody migrant, another one swamping the

31

country. What do we care?' Adam said.

'*He's* a child, Adam, a little boy,' I yelled. 'What's the matter with you?'

'There's plenty more where he came from, coming over here taking our jobs and houses, not our problem.'

'You haven't got a job because you're lazy,' I told him. 'You can't blame this kid for your own idleness.'

'Forget about the kid – think about the *weed*.' Adam snapped. 'We'll make a killing, won't be skint for ages.'

'You're saying we should take the weed – I get that – but what do we do with him?'

'Leave him here. He'll sort himself out.'

'We can't do that, Adam, we don't know how long he's been adrift and he might be sick.' I brushed dark hair off the boy's forehead, his skin now felt hot and clammy as though he had a fever.

'Then he'll die on the beach,' Adam huffed. 'At least he won't be able to grass us up – result.'

'You're a bastard, Adam, you know that don't you?' I hissed angrily.

'Soon to be a *rich* bastard.' He chuckled and rubbed his fingers together.

'Dave's right,' Ben said. 'We've got to help him and if he can't speak English he can't grass us up.'

'I agree with Adam,' Charlie said. 'Save the weed and chuck the kid back.'

'Chuck him back?' I couldn't believe what I'd heard.

'Why not? Just another body washing up on a beach somewhere and one less scrounging migrant over here. He'll probably grow up to be a suicide bomber.'

I looked down at the boy who had shuffled closer to

32

the blazing driftwood, still licking the chocolate wrapper.

'We can't do that,' I said. 'Really we can't. I'm not gonna be part of anything like that, it's way too wrong.'

'You're a pussy,' Adam snarled nastily, 'and I'm not going to let you fuck this up for us. This is the best chance we've ever had, probably never get another.'

'Calm down,' Ben said. 'Why can't we do both? One of us can fetch a car while the others move the gear up behind that big rock. We get the weed away then come back for the kid and take him somewhere safe.'

'Let's boost Dad's car,' Charlie said. 'He's away, so it won't be missed. Come on, Adam.'

'OK. You two move the gear, we'll be back.' They scurried up the beach and were soon lost to the darkness.

The bale was too heavy to move, wrappings soaking wet, so we slit open the thick waterproof covering with Ben's knife and a mass of shrink-wrapped bundles spilled out onto the sand.

I whistled. 'Blimey, Ben, if each one of these is a kilo, Adam's right, we'll be made up – if we can sell it.'

'That won't be a problem, Adam knows people.'

'Yeah, I'll bet he does. I've seen him and Charlie in a different light tonight; nasty racist scrotes. We *must* save the kid, Ben.'

I glanced towards the fire and the boy was watching us with empty eyes. I wasn't sure he was actually seeing anything.

We began moving packages and stashing them behind the rock and soon the bale was light enough to haul up the beach. Hot and sweaty, I went back to the fire to check on the boy. He was still staring into the flames, but he'd stopped shivering. I heard an engine approaching, the headlights snapped off and Adam and Charlie leapt out of a people carrier.

'Get it all moved, lads?' Adam shouted.

'Yeah, it's all here,' I answered.

Charlie opened the back of the minivan and tugged out a wheelie bin.

'Load it in this,' he said, 'and we can push it up to the car. Once it's on board, we can work out what we're going to do with the puking Paki.'

'Don't call him that!' Ben said, angrily.

'He is what he is, you can't deny it,' Charlie snapped back. 'I don't expect anyone's even missing him.'

I ignored them and began filling the bin. It took three trips to load all the weed in the car and soon only the rubber outer covering was left, like an enormous punctured inner tube.

'Best chuck that back,' Charlie said. 'The tide'll take the evidence away.'

'Wrap the kid in it,' Adam muttered darkly, 'two birds – one stone.'

That's when I hit him; a swift chop to the throat and he went down gasping and retching, clutching at his neck, unable to speak. I managed to kick him satisfyingly in the ribs before the others dragged me away.

'Christ, Dave, what do you think you're doing?' Ben shouted.

'We are *not*, definitely *not* throwing that kid back into the sea. How can you even *think* such a thing? You're a nasty bastard, Adam. I want nothing more to do with you.'

Adam sat up, holding his side and rubbing his neck.

'Great,' he croaked. 'That means we'll spilt the profits three ways, more for us. You're a pathetic loser, Dave, always have been and can't see an opportunity when it's dropped in front of you. The kid has seen us – seen what we found. If he grasses, it'll mean prison, long time prison, not a shit and a shave.'

'And if we throw him back into the sea, we'll be committing murder, that's prison too, *life* prison, you muppet.' I yanked my arms away and stormed back towards the fire.

Charlie suddenly lunged at me, grabbed my shoulders, spun me round and planted a vicious head butt on my nose. Blood poured down my chin and splashed on the sand.

The boy looked up at me with huge, brown eyes full of reflected flames and horror. My heart ached for him. How far had he travelled? Where was his home? Were his family on board the boat that capsized? They must have been; why else would he be on his own? I sat by the fire and put an arm round Amraz, trying to staunch the flow of blood from my nose. Ben stood behind me.

'We're taking the weed to town; Adam knows a guy.'

'You said,' I muttered.

'Are you coming?'

'I'm not leaving the boy.'

'What are you going to do?'

'Take him somewhere safe.'

'Where?' Ben persisted.

'I don't know! Why don't you just piss off with the Brothers Grimm and leave us alone. This is not your problem and you don't *really* care, so get lost, Ben.'

35

'You better keep this quiet, mate,' he said. 'If news of this gets out, you know they'll come after you.'

I heard him scuff away through the sand. The car started and headlights swept the cove before it turned towards town.

The fire had burnt down and the night was cold. The boy began to shiver again, so I pulled him to his feet and headed up the beach. We had a long walk before we reached the police substation on the edge of the town. There was a light showing inside, but the door was locked. I hammered on the painted wood and it eventually swung open. A wary uniformed copper peered into the night.

'What do you want?' he grouched, eyes fixing on my bloodied nose.

I pushed Amraz into the light spilling from the doorway. 'I've found this boy on the beach; I think he's a migrant.'

The cop opened the door wider and regarded us from under bushy eyebrows.

'You better come in,' he said reluctantly.

We followed him to an office where he sat us at a table and brewed tea. The boy gratefully wrapped his hands around the hot mug, still desperate for warmth. I wondered how long he'd been in the water and how he'd managed to survive.

The officer flipped open a pad, scribbled down my details and listened as I spun a story that I'd been on the beach *on my own* and the boy waded out of the water.

'He says his name is Amraz, drew a picture of a boat in the sand. I think it might have capsized, but I'm not sure.'

36

'Amraz,' the officer repeated, scribbling on the pad.

'Amraz,' the boy said, pointing to his chest. 'I, Amraz. Kurdiss refugee. Famlee dead. Amraz alone.'

I stared at him in amazement. 'You can speak English?'

'Small Engliss.' He patted my arm and almost smiled. 'This man – *good* man. Friends *bad* men. I tell about *bad* men.'

MAKING A KILLING

When Lily woke, her head was full of murderous thoughts, not the left over wisps of nightmares, but certain knowledge she was going to kill someone. She knew who and why, but not how.

Unsurprisingly, she hadn't killed anyone before and had no clue how to commit a murder. She took the day off, informed her boss she was sick. He sounded disgruntled, but Lily didn't care, she was due some compassionate leave.

She brewed coffee, carried it to her cramped home-office and switched on the computer. The screensaver floated in front of her eyes and she smiled at the photo of her sister on a camel outside The Treasury in the ancient city of Petra. For her sister – another Petra – it had been the trip of a lifetime. Her face was happy, beautiful, no sign of the disease she no doubt had. She died from cancer three weeks ago and Lily missed her constantly.

She stared at the keyboard wondering what to type into the search engine, 'How to murder someone', seemed like a bad idea. Everyone knew there was no such thing as online privacy and she didn't want to get caught *before* the murder, but didn't much care if she was caught *after.*

She began by researching fatal injuries. Head wounds inflicted with blunt instruments, traffic accidents, falls, death from shooting injuries, stabbings, drowning, asphyxiation, poisoning, the list was endless. She waded through internet dross and realised killing someone wasn't easy. She couldn't stab anyone, or hold them underwater like a newborn kitten, or force a plastic bag over their head until they suffocated and wasn't sure she had what it took to murder another human being.

Lily wondered about hiring a hit man and made a few tentative forays into the area online. Most of what she discovered related to movies and video games, not that she was surprised. She'd have been *more* surprised if hiring an assassin was as easy as ordering groceries.

She made lunch and tried to think about something else, but couldn't. The murderous feeling she had woken up with grew stronger and she knew there was no easy solution. She wanted someone dead and would have to do it herself. How would it feel to be a murderer she wondered? Would she be wracked with guilt for the rest of her life, or would she feel relieved?

Lily returned to her office and lifted the dictionary down from the bookcase. The entry for murder read, 'The unlawful and premeditated killing of a human being by another.' What she was planning was certainly unlawful, but she felt this was a justified killing – not murder.

She considered tampering with her victim's car. It worked well enough in films – cut the brake pipes and the driver loses control on a steep gradient before plunging over a cliff; but this was *real* life. There was no guarantee her victim would drive near a cliff or fast enough to cause a serious accident. He might use the car in town and brake failure would only generate a minor accident, not death; and of course there were other people to consider. She didn't want to be responsible for a pile-up on the motorway.

The only method she could seriously consider was pushing her victim off somewhere high. There would be blood, but she wouldn't see it. Her only input would be a swift shove and *knew* she could do that. As long as the drop was high enough, death would be certain and she wouldn't have to check the body. Local media was bound to report the incident – a bonus if they called it suicide.

The next day Lily researched high places, cliffs, towers, bridges and hit an unexpected snag. Most were designed to be anti-suicide and those that hadn't been designed that way, had nets and barriers retro-fitted to make jumping impossible. Even if she found a suitable venue, how could she lure her victim there?

She plotted all day, examined many different scenarios and by evening, had a plan. She called her victim and the phone rang a long time before it was answered.

'Alexander James,' said a deep voice, as smooth as melted chocolate.

'Hi, Alex. It's Lily, Petra's sister.'

'Lily! Lovely to hear from you. How are you?'

'Not bad, under the circumstances.'

'I heard about Petra,' he said, oozing sympathy. 'I'm *so* sorry I didn't get to the funeral. Did everything go OK?'

'As well as a funeral can; a good turnout.'

'Did the flowers arrive?' he asked.

'Yes, thank you, they were lovely.'

The conversation stalled and the silence lengthened.

'Well,' he said, 'it's good to hear from you.'

Lily knew he was going to end the call and panicked.

'Are you free tomorrow evening?' she asked. 'Petra left a letter with her will, bequeathing small items to people who meant something to her and your name is on the list.'

'Really?' he said. 'I'm touched. Let me check my diary, hang on.'

She waited.

He came back on the line. 'I *am* free tomorrow. What do you have in mind?'

'How about dinner, the French place in town, seven-thirty?'

'Perfect,' he said. 'Would you like a lift, or shall I meet you there?'

'I'll meet you there.'

Lily took a long time getting ready. She wanted to look smart, but blend in and the clothes needed to be practical, easy to move in. She settled for smart trousers and jacket, ankle boots and a bright scarf, and left her dark hair loose so it hung round her face, partially obscuring her features making her look generic and unmemorable.

A taxi delivered Lily to the restaurant a few minutes early. Alexander arrived shortly after and she watched him weave his way towards her. He was an attractive charismatic man dressed in an expensive hand-tailored suit with patent leather shoes that shone like obsidian. His hair was dark and curly, his eyes blue. A deep scar lined his left cheek and seemed to enhance his appearance. Lily understood why her sister had been drawn to him, especially when she was so ill and clutching at straws.

He smiled: 'Lily, you look *lovely*,' he gushed.

She held out her hand, he raised it to his mouth and kissed it. She resisted the urge to shudder, detested the wetness of his lips on her skin.

'Thank you,' she said. 'You scrub up well too.'

He laughed, settling in the chair opposite. 'Have to make an effort when dining with a beautiful woman.'

He was so sleazy-predictable that Lily was heartened. This evening's business was going to be easier than she thought.

Alex ordered for them both. Lily hoped he was going to pay, she didn't want to waste a single penny on this detestable creep. If it hadn't been for him, her sister might still be alive. She flirted outrageously and he basked in the attention. They talked about stuff people usually chat about, the weather, work, and current affairs. He was incredibly opinionated and Lily knew he wasn't listening to her. She sat back, let him talk and made sure his wine glass was regularly topped up. She drank little, needed a clear head, but Alex was well down the third bottle. His posture had softened and his words blurred into each other. Lily was encouraged, it was better if he *didn't* have a clear head.

'So,' he slurred, 'you said Petra mentioned me in a letter?'

'That's right. She left instructions for me to deliver small items to her friends and you're on the list. You didn't know her long did you?'

'No,' he admitted, 'I met her after she became ill. A

great loss, she was so young.' He looked mournful, but Lily wasn't fooled.

'She told me you were treating her.'

'It's how we met.' He slurped more wine and I refilled his glass.

'You're a doctor?' I asked.

He shook his head. 'Not in the sense you mean. I'm a healer, I cure cancer.'

'How do you do that?' She pretended ignorance, but knew what he did.

'Cancer is caused by parasites,' he said. 'Conventional medicine has been trying to cure the disease in completely the wrong way. I've developed apparatus that delivers electrical pulses. The pulses upset the internal balance of the parasites and kills them, then the tumour dissolves. I also prescribe natural herbs and homeopathy to strengthen the therapy.'

'Have you cured many?'

'More than I can count,' he boasted. 'It's a wonderful natural treatment, no need for poisonous chemotherapy or painful operations.'

'Is it expensive? Petra never said how much she paid.' Lily knew exactly how much the leech had taken from her sister. She'd seen Petra's bank statements and Alex had taken everything.

'It's not about money though is it?' he said. 'When death threatens, money is the least of your worries, you just want to be healed.'

'So what went wrong? Why did she die?'

His face lost its egotistical smirk and Lily watched him construct a suitable answer.

43

'Didn't start treatment early enough I'm afraid. I *did* think I could help her, but the tumour was too advanced, the parasite count too high. I did my best, but not everything works for everybody.' He checked his watch. 'I must be going I'm afraid, but it's been great to meet you.'

'Let's flag down a cab,' Lily said, 'we can share it. I need to collect the keepsake Petra left for you. It's in her apartment, we can pop in on the way home.'

Petra's apartment was on the top floor and she'd had access to the roof garden. Lily had the key and just needed to coax Alex onto the roof, the rest would be easy.

Nerves hit her in the back of the taxi. It had been torture spending time with the odious man, a man who latched onto people when they were at their lowest, promising a cure before parting them from their money. She leant in close to his ear and he smiled as though he was expecting a kiss. Lily was so angry her temper bubbled to the surface and after all her careful planning, she blew it.

'You killed my sister,' she hissed. 'You pedalled your snake-oil treatment, she fell for it and died. How do you live with yourself?'

He recoiled: 'That's not true. I've cured many people. If your sister had come to me sooner . . . '

'Don't you *dare* make this her fault. You and your kind should be shot. She'd be alive today if she hadn't met you.'

Shockingly, she lashed out at Alex with her fist and caught him on the side of his head.

'Driver, stop the car!' he yelled. 'I'm getting out. She's a mad woman.'

44

Her plan had disintegrated. She'd never get him up to the apartment now. All that plotting for nothing. She grabbed his arm as the taxi slowed and hung on, trying to prevent him leaving. He fought back, opening the door with one hand, while trying to wrench his arm from her grasp. He was suddenly free and scrambled out.

There was a thud, the crunch of metal on metal, the shattering of glass. Lily covered her face. When she uncovered it, she saw the door had been ripped off and Alex had vanished. The cab driver ran into the road and wailed. Lily slid across the back seat and peered out. Alex was lying crumpled on the tarmac and a van was slewed across the road. A small crowd was gathering, everyone staring at the body on the ground, no one was looking in her direction.

She quietly opened the remaining back door, slipped out unnoticed into the night, and made her way home through dark streets. She turned on her computer, gazed at the screensaver, at her beautiful sister and for the first time since her death, her emotions calmed. She took a deep breath and smiled.

STILL WATERS

I found Mum in the nook overlooking the koi pond. She sat there for hours every day whether or not it was raining, protected by a vaguely hobbit-like shelter dug into the bank. Today the sun was shining, reflections from the pool illuminated her face and I was shocked to see that she suddenly looked old. She spotted me and waved.

'My darling girl,' she called. 'You're early.'

I picked my way along the narrow gravel path and squeezed into the nook. Mum kissed my cheek so gently it felt as though my skin had been brushed by a moth's wing.

'You called – I came,' I said. 'Everything OK?'

'Does there have to be something wrong for you to visit your mother?' she teased.

'Of course not.' I watched the fish swirl beneath the surface, sunshine ricocheting off their scales in a dazzling display. I threw a few pellets into the water and the greedy creatures slurped enthusiastically.

The pool had been Dad's idea – I remember him digging. It seemed as though he spent all his spare time out in the garden with a shovel. He let me help sometimes, not that a five year old was very productive, but he gave me a tiny shovel and a sandcastle bucket and I laboured by his side. Then, one morning when I woke up, Mum told me he had gone away and I didn't see him again. It was shocking to lose him when I was so young. It felt as though he'd died. I had tried to trace him, clandestinely of course, Mum wouldn't have approved, but each time I tried I ran into a dead end. Even the Salvation Army had drawn a blank.

Mum's fierce independence served her well and after the dust settled, she continued building the pool. She bought a cement mixer and spent many weekends mixing and spreading, shaping and contouring. The completed pond was so large it took days to fill using the hose. I remember she was nervous because we didn't have a hosepipe licence and our neighbour was a local councillor.

Once the pond had been filled and left for a month to, "settle in" as Mum told me, we visited an aquatic centre and bought water lilies and oxygenating weed. We waited another month before returning to choose the fish. We picked out twenty, young koi carp about four inches long and the day we released them into their new home had always been one of my happiest childhood memories. The fish were now two feet long and all had names. Mum fed them by hand every day, smiling as they kissed morsels of food from her fingers, before flipping their beautiful tails and swimming away under the lily pads; slow motion, underwater fireworks.

Mum poured two mugs of coffee from the cafetiere that was always close to hand.

'I have something to tell you,' she said.

'Is it Dad?' I asked. 'Has he been in touch?'

She chuckled. 'He's been gone thirty years, what makes you think he'd suddenly contact me?'

'He might,' I huffed.

'He won't,' she said. 'I don't know why you keep

47

thinking like this. You need to move on, I have.'

'He's my dad,' I said. 'I'd like to know where he is.'

She sighed: 'No, darling girl, I haven't heard from him.'

'So what then?'

She gazed at the fish, but I don't think she was seeing them.

'I'm not very well,' she muttered. 'Haven't been for a while. Liver cancer the doctor says, so I won't be around much longer.'

I felt as though someone had whacked me in the stomach with a sledgehammer and gasped for air.

'Cancer?' my voice wavered. 'Can they do anything?'

'Not really, no,' she said. 'Certainly nothing I want them to. I don't want to spend my last months plugged into a machine being given hefty doses of chemo, can't see the point, so I've told them I'm refusing treatment. Pain management only and no resuscitation rubbish.'

'Are you sure? There are some amazing new treatments these days and the chemo's better, it doesn't always make you go bald.'

I ran my fingers through her long hair, she snagged my hand and squeezed it.

'Did they tell you how long?' I asked as tears formed in my eyes. I couldn't imagine how I could survive the rest of my life without Mum in it. We'd always been so close, probably due to Dad's abandonment, there was only us. No aunties or uncles and no grandparents. I was an only child from a long line of only children.

'Couple of months if I'm lucky,' she said, 'but what does it matter? We all die. *How* is more important than

48

when, surely.'

'Let's get a second opinion.'

'No point. Anyway, we have a much bigger problem.'

'We do?' I couldn't think what could be bigger.

Mum nodded gravely: 'The pond is leaking.'

'What?'

'The pond. It sprang a leak during the winter and needs repairing urgently. I'm keeping it topped up with the hose, but that can't go on forever, tap water's not wonderful for the fish. It's going to be a massive job, I think the bottom has cracked.'

I didn't know what to say so let her chatter on. Why on earth was she worrying about the pond? Surely her health problems were more pressing.

'I'll have to get someone in,' she was saying. 'I've found somewhere for the fish – like kennels – so they can come back when the work's finished.'

'Why not leave the pond, Mum. It's a lot of unnecessary hassle, especially now. You've other things to think about.'

'My darling girl, if you think I'm going to spend the next two months mooning around contemplating my death, you are *very* much mistaken. And what about the poor fish? No, the pond needs fixing and I need a project. I won't be doing any of the work myself, but I shall oversee it. Can't trust builders to do anything properly.'

A few days later the pool men arrived, two workers from the aquatic centre where we'd bought the fish so long ago. They slowly drained the water, netted the fish and dispatched them to their temporary home. I spent hours huddled in the nook with mum watching them work. It was more entertaining than television and gave me a good excuse to keep an eye on her as the cancer shrank her body before my eyes.

As soon as the pool was empty it became obvious the problem was more serious than a crack; the decision was made to remove and replace the concrete liner. Planks were laid at one end of the pool and a mini digger driven in to break up the bottom. Mum sat in the nook drinking coffee and frowning.

'You OK, Mum?'

'I'm fine, but don't like seeing the digger smash up the pool.'

I remembered something, the flash of a memory from long ago, fleeting and I missed it.

'Why does it bother you?' I asked.

'No reason really.'

The memory appeared again. This time I snagged it and pictures flooded into my mind; arguments between my parents, raised voices, Mum crying. I remembered Dad digging the pond realising he hadn't dug in his spare time, but in his unhappy times. Another darker memory swirled in my head like a fish and I shuddered.

'Are you worried what they might find?' I asked.

'What? No – I'm remembering how much work it was to lay the concrete, months of cracked hands and broken nails and it's being ripped out in minutes.'

'I told Mrs Bees you buried Dad under the pond.' Words flew out before I could stop them.

Mum stared at me. 'Mrs Bees? Your primary school teacher? What did she say?' A smile danced on her lips.

'That I was being silly. Said he'd left home.' I paused, wondering how much to tell her. 'Mrs Bees said you'd *told* Dad to leave. Did you?'

'Do we have to talk about this now?'

'Don't you think we should, and if not now – when?'

Mum sighed: 'Yes, my darling girl, I told him to go. He wasn't good for either of us.'

'So *you* say, but I was only five. I didn't get asked. How was it better for me to grow up without him?'

'Trust me – it was.'

'But what did he do?' I persisted.

'He wasn't a good husband.'

'Not a good husband? What do you mean?'

'He had affairs, he drank too much and he gambled; the three deadly sins. Is that what you wanted to hear? You were too small to understand what was going on, but I *knew* he was no good.'

A shout from the excavation dragged our attention back to the garden. The digger was silent and the men were scrabbling about in the shattered concrete. I left the nook and stood on the edge gazing down at the rubble.

'What is it?' I called.

'Not sure, the bucket snagged on something.'

I glanced at Mum, but she didn't seem interested. I walked to the end of the pool and jumped down into the pit.

'You mustn't come down here,' one of the men said. 'Health and safety rules don't allow it.'

'I want to know what you've found.'

'Probably nothing, but you must get out and when we've dug it up, we'll show you. Please, it's not safe.'

51

I climbed out and tucked back into the nook with Mum. The sun vanished behind a cloud and a few drops of rain fell, my mood matched the weather.

'What's down there, Mum?'

'How would I know?'

'You built the bloody pool. *Is* Dad down there?'

She looked shocked, clasped a hand to her mouth like a child who'd been caught misbehaving . . . then she laughed. She tossed her head back and roared and even though I didn't know why she was laughing, I joined in – so did the workmen.

Eventually she regained control and asked: 'You really thought Dad was under the pool?'

I nodded: 'Yes, I really thought he was under the pool.'

That set her off again until she could hardly breathe.

The men finally extricated a six foot length of old drainage pipe from the hole and a few weeks later the new pool had been filled with water and planted with lilies. The fish were due at the weekend and we were looking forward to their arrival.

Mum had faded during the last month. Her skin looked as though cling film had been stretched over it and she lost weight rapidly. I moved in and she protested, but life was too difficult for her now without help.

On Saturday the animal ambulance arrived with the koi on board in large, temperature controlled tanks. Mum wanted to check them over before they were released and we helped her climb in the back of the van. I heard her cooing over her pets, giggling like a child as they kissed her fingers. The sound made me smile, she was happy.

The fish were netted, gently lowered into their new pool and they swirled in the water exploring. I wondered if they remembered they were here before, or whether koi and goldfish shared a poor memory – and wondered at my own. How *could* I have thought Dad was buried under the pool? I chuckled.

'What?' Mum asked.

'Me, accusing you of murdering Dad. I can't *believe* I told Mrs Bees you had, it makes my toes curl.'

'It is pretty funny. Good thing you didn't remember it until now, something like that would have been awful during puberty,' she giggled.

We drank coffee and watched the fish.

'This is my second happiest memory,' I said. 'Releasing the fish today has been lovely, just like it was when we first bought them. I almost feel five again.'

'I wish I did,' Mum muttered and hauled herself to her feet. 'It's getting cold, let's go in and give the fish some privacy.'

Mum died two days later and I miss her. It's that simple, I *miss* her. I've missed her every day she's been gone and so far it hasn't got any easier. Mum's solicitor arrived at ten this morning with a briefcase full of documents and a folder full of forms. I rummaged through the pile and discovered the old deeds packet. I love old maps and documents and flicked through the yellowing paper finding boundary maps, sewage pipe records and details of past owners. Near the back was a hand drawn plan of the property, house and garden. The address was written on the bottom right hand corner and my mother's signature appeared by the side. Something had originally been stapled to the plan, I could see two holes in the paper, but I had no clue what.

I handed it to the solicitor: 'What's this?'

He peered at it, turned it over, turned it back and peered some more before ferreting about in the deeds and extracting a sheet of paper.

'Ah, yes, thought so,' he said. '*Notification of Home Burial*. There's a grave behind the garage.'

MAKING A DIFFERENCE

The attempted hanging was the reason I left; although – truthfully – it wasn't the hanging, it was what came after.

I was working nights and at 2am Cilla and I went on the usual walkabout. At the junction of corridors Cilla turned left to check the cells, I turned right and headed towards the common areas.

I wandered through the association room, nostrils flinching at the smell of tobacco, cannabis and institution. On the far side the bathrooms, disinfectant, urine and worse. Entering the shower area I walked into a pair of feet level with my face and forgot to fill my lungs. A girl – no more than twenty – swung from a grubby towelling belt twisted around her neck, secured to a light fitting.

A sanitary disposal bin lay on its side. I placed it upright, climbed on top and used a cut-down tool to sever the material. I couldn't hold her, she slipped through my arms and landed on the damp tiles like a wet sack; I recognised Julie Canavan. Slapping the panic button on the wall, I dropped to the floor and began CPR.

Water soaked through the knees of my trousers, bones jammed painfully on the tiles. The bell jangled my nerves, I tried to block out the racket and concentrated on chest compressions, one, two, three, four . . . New sounds, the mass rattle of bunches of keys, a multitude of squeaky thumping footfalls as staff ran towards me.

'Who is it?' someone asked.

I ignored the question, busy trying to save the young life beneath me.

The Principal Officer arrived and barked orders to his subordinates: 'Call an ambulance; keep the prisoners in their cells; cordon off the area; kill the alarm.'

I bounced up and down, hands clasped as though in prayer, mind churning a desperate mantra; 'Don't die – *breathe*. Don't die – *breathe*.' I blew two rescue breaths into Julie's mouth, watched her chest rise and began pumping again.

My head swam with dizziness, heat seared my skin, sweat trickled between my shoulder blades and still she lay motionless.

'How long?' the PO asked.

'At least five,' Cilla answered. 'Maybe longer.'

I continued compressions, aware of the conversation, knowing time was passing and when I next blew into the slack mouth felt resistance. I backed away as Julie snatched a breath and suddenly sat up to vomit on the tiles.

Her eyes focussed, opened wide and she took in the scene, horror on her face. Her body suddenly arched, she flung herself backwards and her skull hit the floor, the sound of a breaking egg shell. Blood seeped from between strands of blond hair, mingled with the puddles, surrounded her like a halo and she was still. I stared at her feeling an unreasonable outrage. Why would she *do* that? The pool of blood blossomed and her skin paled further; she resembled a contemporary Ophelia, beautiful and tragic.

Strong hands grabbed my arms and dragged me away, knees skinned by the hard floor as I was hauled upright. Two paramedics rushed in as I was ushered from the room, one officer pulling, Cilla shoving from behind.

'Come away now, Kim,' the PO said. 'Let the guys deal with this.'

They shepherded me to the office. A hot sweet mug of tea appeared and lifting it to my lips I saw how badly my hands were shaking. The PO sat opposite, pen poised, incident form on the desk.

'So, tell me, Kim,' he said. 'What happened?'

I told him how I'd found Julie hanging from the light fitting, cut her down and tried to save her life, succeeded too, but the blood disturbed me. I knew Julie had wounded herself purposely. I didn't know why.

'You should go home,' the boss said. 'We have your statement and you need time to process. Take a couple of days.'

The door banged open and a green clad medic entered looking grim. My boss raised his eyebrows in a question.

'We're taking her in,' the medic said. 'Possible skull fracture, damage to her windpipe and blood loss.'

'Is she conscious?' I asked.

'Barely. We need an escort.'

'I'll go.' I leapt up and Cilla tried to stop me. I angrily shook off her hands. 'I'm going,' I said and glared at the boss until he nodded reluctantly.

'OK, but you'd be better off at home,' he mumbled.

I shook my head.

'Then take Cilla with you,' he said. 'Keep in touch.'

58

I climbed in the back of the ambulance and held Julie's hand, it was damp and frigid, like the skin of a dead person, but I heard shallow breathing under the mask and her eyelids flickered. She didn't wake up.

As soon as we left the prison grounds the driver hit the siren and we sped through early morning streets. The vehicle rolled around bends, I felt nauseous and lowered my head.

'You OK?' the medic asked.

'Fine,' I lied, willing the journey to end.

Julie was in bed, head bandaged, drips and tubes snaked from beneath the hospital gown. Machines bleeped and whirred and I sat by her bed watching, waiting.

Nurses came and went, the day shift clocked on and Julie remained unresponsive. Cilla told me I should go home but I refused. It wasn't until midmorning I noticed signs of consciousness and felt Julie's fingers twitch in mine. Slowly she returned to the world, confused, frightened and I tried to calm her.

'Hey, sunshine,' I said. 'Welcome back. You're safe. You're in hospital and you're going to be fine.'

She turned to look at me, opened her mouth as if to speak but made no sound.

'It's OK. Don't try to talk. The doctors say you've damaged your windpipe and spilt your head open, but no fracture. You'll be right as rain in a few days.'

A nurse floated in, checked the drips and machines, smiled at me nervously – the uniform didn't encourage friendliness – then left in search of the doctor. I squeezed Julie's hand gently, felt her try to pull away and let go.

She opened her mouth again and I leaned closer.

'Why?' she creaked.

'Why what?'

'Why did you cut me down?'

My answer was immediate: 'To save your life.'

Julie swallowed painfully and closed her eyes: 'Who asked you?'

'Well . . . no one. It was the right thing to do.'

Julie groaned and shook her head.

'Of *course* it was,' I said. 'You have your life ahead of you and you're due for release in two weeks. You'll be home soon.'

She turned her face away and I didn't know what to do, what to say, anything. Finally she looked back and fixed me with red rimmed eyes full of tears and pleading – I didn't know what for. I gripped her hand.

'You're going home, Julie,' I said. 'You won't go back to jail, you'll be released from hospital as soon as you're well enough.'

A desert-dry sob lodged in her throat. She took a deep breath and wheezed: 'You had no right. You should have let me die.'

'No, that's never the answer, you know that.'

'Better than sending me back to my *father*.' She loaded his name with hate and exhausted, turned to the wall and said nothing more.

Her words landed in my heart like a punch and knowing instinctively what they meant, I stood, knocked over the plastic chair and fled.

At HMP Heatherlea I changed out of my uniform, wrote a hasty letter of resignation and walked away, sick with myself and the system; the useless, unfit-for-purpose system that imprisoned vulnerable and abused women. Julie Canavan's dreadful story wasn't the first I'd heard, but it would be the last I'd hear in a prison.

Many weeks crawled by filled with too many sleepless nights and too much self-medication; sleeping pills, booze and the odd spliff. I drifted, lost in the world, purposeless, but it was better than being part of a failing institution.

The first month I shut myself away. I couldn't get Julie out of my mind; Julie hanging; Julie dying on the wet tiles; Julie's blood from the self-inflicted wound and what she'd said, 'back to my father.' The words wouldn't leave, refused to be buried or locked away in a mental strong-box and swam in my soul. I asked Cilla to give me Julie's home address so I could visit, make sure she was safe, but she refused and quoted the rules. I tried to track the girl down myself – and failed.

The second month I continued to worry about her and concocted different scenarios, alternative endings to her story – so many I could have filled the pages of a novel.

The third month I returned to dark brooding and think I would have stayed in that place forever if Cilla hadn't encouraged me back to reality. She gave me a leaflet explaining how I could volunteer to work for the Samaritans, convinced me I'd be good at it. I applied and Cilla was right. I had a purpose again.

I quickly became addicted to the work and never had any trouble meeting the minimum hours, in fact I volunteered for more – as many as I could within the guidelines and chose nightshifts. The road outside the office was quiet after midnight, hardly any traffic; the occasional siren in the distance, a drunk serenading himself as he staggered home.

It was best when it was just me and whoever called in. The disturbed, the bereaved, the indebted, the caught out – any number of reasons made people consider suicide. I liked to think the lucky ones called the helpline and tried to imagine their eventual outcomes. It wasn't difficult to convince myself that *here* I made a difference, not as a prison officer in a jail. The penal system prevented anyone making a difference. Understaffed, under-resourced and underpaid. We were little more than zoo keepers, ensuring our charges stayed in their cages, were fed and watered and didn't kill each other.

I made a fresh pot of coffee and stood at the window to watch the street. I spotted a scruffy town fox slip from between a cluster of bins and trot down the centre of the road, two mangy felines eyed the hunter warily until it vanished beneath a fence. The phones had been quiet tonight, two pranksters, an elderly woman who wanted to know how to change a fuse and two silent calls. It was those that stopped me sleeping by wriggling into my brain as successfully as silent earworms, putting down strong roots. The phone rang, I sat behind the desk, took a deep, calming breath and picked up the receiver.

'Hello, this is the Samaritans.'

Silence. I repeated my greeting but apart from labored breathing, I heard nothing. I waited then said: 'I'm still here. Would you like to talk to me?'

No answer. More breathing. More waiting. I tried a different approach.

'Are you thinking of taking your life?'

I thought I heard a sob, maybe a sniffle – something.

'I won't hang up on you, but it would be good to talk.'

I heard throat clearing, then: 'Hello?' A woman, young.

'Hi there,' I said. 'My name's Kim. Can you tell me what's on your mind?'

'I . . . I don't know . . . it's all such a mess.' Her voice sounded weirdly familiar.

'No rush, we have plenty of time.'

A long pause, then: 'Can I ask . . . is your name Kim Jefferies?'

My mind juddered: 'Oh God, Julie?'

'Yes, Miss, it's me! What are you doing there?'

'I'm a volunteer. I'm not at the prison any more, I left after . . .'

There was more silence before she asked: 'Can we meet? Talk face to face? You could come to my house.'

'It's not allowed, I . . .'

'*Please.* Things are *really* bad for me and it's your fault. You *must* come.'

'How is it my fault?' I stammered, still trying to get my head around the coincidence, not convinced Julie hadn't engineered this and wondered if that was even possible.

'Because you saved my life. If it wasn't for you I'd be dead and the shit wouldn't be happening.'

Reluctantly I agreed, noted down her address and

arranged to meet when my shift ended and her father had left for the job centre.

I'd been there an hour listening to Julie tell me that fate was another word for coincidence and we were obviously destined to meet, when there was a rattle towards the back of the house. Julie sat up straight and her hands began to tremble followed by the rest of her.

An angry voice broke the silence: 'Jules? Where the fuck are you?'

Footsteps outside the door before it was flung wide and a glowering man stood in the opening. He was dressed in a dirty track suit – although the only track it had ever seen was probably the dogs – and a grubby white tee shirt, food spills down the front, an accumulation on the belly shelf. Gawking at him I knew Julie had never stood a chance.

'Bringing friends home?' he sneered. 'You know the rules, *no* friends.'

Julie flinched and a tic twitched one cheek. Her father turned his attention on me. A sticky tongue flicked lizard-like between unshaven lips sounding like sandpaper on rusty metal. My insides cringed. I didn't like the way he was looking at me.

'She's a bit old for me,' he grumbled, 'but I guess you've told her the house rules.'

He took a step towards me.

'No, Dad!' Julie yelled. He silenced her with a backhander, I felt blood splash my skin, and I lost it – properly lost it.

I flew at him, punched him hard in the midriff,

scraped his shin with the side of my boot and stamped viciously on the top of his foot. He staggered back howling in pain, his enormous weight off balance and danced a few tottery baby steps before he fell. The back of a dining chair broke his fall – and his neck and he stopped breathing.

I was horrified, couldn't make sense of what had happened. I'd just killed a man, *me*, an ex-prison officer, serving Samaritan and I'd caused a death.

Julie shook my arm: 'Miss, snap out of it. We can't leave him here, we've gotta move the body.'

'No, we can't do that. We must call the police, tell them what happened, self-defence compounded by an unlucky fall.'

'Miss, no! You're an ex-screw, I'm an ex-con. We shouldn't be seen together and definitely not with a dead man, even if he is a monster.'

'We can explain, they . . .'

'Won't believe us,' she finished. 'So help me lose him.'

'Where do you *lose* a body?'

'Shouldn't be too difficult. He's not bleeding so all we have to do is get him away from the house; make sure there are no clues on the body; cut his fingers off . . .'

'Wait a bloody minute,' I protested.

'The longer it takes to identify him the better. There's some plastic in the garage. We'll wrap him up, put him in the car, drive him a few miles away and dump him.'

I couldn't believe the change in Julie from a frightened victim to a powerful, dangerous woman. Her new personality swept me along and she convinced me her plan was the best option. We donned rubber gloves, hauled him to the car, posted him in the boot and Julie dropped a pair of bolt cutters on his chest. Bile rose to my mouth.

'We shouldn't be doing this.'

'Miss – we already are. Now get in and drive!'

Two hours later we arrived at a patch of dense woodland somewhere in Mid-Wales. Julie was all business. She dragged a wheelbarrow from the back seat and together we rolled her father inside. She told me to put carrier bags on my feet and like CSI in reverse, we pushed the body into the darkest part of the forest. Julie picked up the bolt cutters and smashed the heavy tool into her father's face over and over again.

'Stop! For God's sake stop.' I begged.

She calmly informed me that smashing his teeth was easier than cutting off his head and I escaped, galloped down the track to the car. I understood how she felt. She was glad her father was dead, but she didn't kill him, I did. All she did was vent her anger and frustration on a dead man who had abused her all her life. In her position I might well have done the same, but it was me who killed him – indirectly and in self-defence – but I took his life and didn't recognise myself anymore.

Eventually Julie reappeared, climbed in the car and we returned to her house to make certain we hadn't left any clues for the police to find. We'd planned to wait a couple of days then report him missing, but unluckily, a neighbour had seen us loading his body in the car.

I put down the pen and looked up: 'I'm done,' I said. 'That's all there is.'

My solicitor smiled, put the statement in her briefcase and patted the back of my hand.

'Hang in there, Kim,' she said. 'I'll soon have you out of here, I promise.'

MEASURE ONCE - CUT TWICE

I am *so* fed up with this. For the last three days I've been traipsing along dark city streets in search of clean, heavy-duty sheets of cardboard. Trudie and I have collected a good pile this evening and if I never have to wade through another mound of soggy October leaves I'll be delighted.

'Come on, Trudie, that's plenty, surely,' I grumbled. 'We won't be able to carry any more. Let's call it a night – please?'

'If we don't go back with enough, Magda will moan at us. You know what she's like, Emma.'

'She'll moan anyway; bloody Moaning Magda. Why isn't she helping?'

'You know why, she's working on the coffin.'

Our mutual friend, Helena, had died a week ago and left a long list of last requests including being cremated in a cardboard coffin, not an off-the-shelf model, but one we'd make ourselves using recycled materials. That's why Trudie and I were tramping wet autumn streets and pinching cardboard from recycling heaps on the pavements, before the bin-men collected it in the morning.

'I'm freezing and my feet are wet,' I whinged. 'Please let's go back. I'm sure this lot will satisfy Magda and if it doesn't, she can find some more herself.'

I didn't wait for Trudie's agreement, but surged up the road trying to keep hold of slippery cardboard and wishing I'd brought some string to hold it all together. Longer arms would have helped enormously.

For most, building a functioning coffin would have been a challenge, but we were a band of committed crafters. Magda worked with glass, Trudie was an expert in cold cast bronze, I made dolls houses and Helena had been an inspired jeweller. We were used to constructing things from scratch and with Magda in charge, nothing could go wrong – she wouldn't let it.

We'd met twenty years ago at Art College and remained good friends although – since Helena's death – Magda had been starting to annoy me. She was tall, statuesque, with a mane of red hair, green eyes, a quick temper synonymous with redheads and a proper fairy-dust and rainbows, dippy-hippy. Everything in Magda's world was *amazing* or *fabulous,* an eternal, over-the-top optimist. She was also a grade one control freak and the older she got, the more controlling she became. I often thought it was a good job she'd remained single. A husband would never have put up with her and, in the absence of one, she tried to control the lives of everyone around her and that usually meant us.

It took an age to trudge back to Magda's place. Trudie booted the bottom of the door to announce our arrival, unwilling to let go of her bundle and Magda opened up. We shuffled along the hall and into the conservatory at the back, dropping our burdens gratefully.

'I hope this is enough,' I said. 'It's starting to drizzle again and soggy cardboard will be useless.'

'Looks *great!*' Magda enthused, the only person I

knew who spoke in italics. 'I've already cut the baseboard *and* a set of paper templates, so it shouldn't take long to put together. I discovered some *lovely* fabric in the garage we can use for the lining, old tents salvaged from Glastonbury last year, every colour you can think of – and some you can't.' She chuckled: 'Dear Helena can rest in a *beautiful* rainbow bower.'

I rolled my eyes at Trudie and looked away, trying hard not to laugh. Magda didn't like people laughing at her.

'Any chance of a cuppa?' I asked. 'It's bloody miserable out there, I can't feel my feet, or my fingers.'

'You know where the kitchen is, Emma, help yourself. I don't want to lose my creative momentum.'

I shrugged out of my coat and stomped off to make coffee. Waiting for the water to boil, I listened to Magda laying down the law.

'No, no, no! Not like that. Give me the stapler. Like *this.*'

I smiled. To the rest of the world, Magda came across as a caring, sparkling individual, full of fun and life and beautiful things, but her close friends knew her for what she really was – horribly insecure. I carried the mugs to the conservatory, plonked them on a side table and picked up a sketch of the proposed casket carefully mapped out in black ink. It didn't look much like a coffin to me.

'Is this what you're planning?' I asked.

'Yes, *gorgeous* isn't it?' Magda enthused.

'Certainly different. What are these bits poking up at the ends?'

'I've based the structure on a *magnificent* Egyptian funeral barge and plan to paint Isis on the sides, wings outstretched to protect our *beloved* friend on her last, spiritual journey.'

I stifled a giggle, buried my face in a mug of coffee and watched as Magda buzzed around the construction, issuing orders to the long-suffering Trudie.

'Hold this will you? Not like that, like *this*. It's bloody *obvious*.'

I was reluctant to join the fray and grateful when I heard the doorbell ring.

'That'll be Spencer,' Magda said. 'Let him in can you, Emma? He's coming to talk about the streaming.'

'The what?' I asked, heading for the front door.

'We're going to live-stream the service so everyone *everywhere* can be part of our celebration for Helena's beautiful life,' Magda gushed.

Opening the door, I was met by a short, scruffy hippy, loaded down with laptops and other assorted bits of kit. I held the door open wide.

'We're out the back, go on through. Would you like some coffee?'

He grunted and shuffled along the hall to the construction site.

'Spencer!' I heard Magda exclaim. '*Wonderful* you could make it. Can you be self-sufficient? I've got my hands rather full. No, Trudie! Use the box cutter and the impact glue, how many times . . .'

We delivered the coffin containing Helena to the crematorium the day before the service, the only day

Magda could arrange a van. I must admit the finished coffin was stunning. The goddess Isis unfurled her wings to encompass the body of our friend and the casket did look remarkably like an Egyptian funeral barge – without the oars. Once it was safely unloaded and placed in a side room, we parted company and arranged to gather again the following afternoon for what Magda had christened, "The Celebration of the Spirit", so I was surprised to hear her voice on the phone later that evening.

'Emma, good you're in. Something *horrendous* has happened. We have to go to the crematorium, *urgently,* and can you pick Trudie up on the way?'

'What's wrong?' I asked.

'No time to explain. Just get there – *yesterday!'*

'I reckon it's fallen to bits,' Trudie said, as I pulled into the car park. 'Magda won't like that, she thinks she's so brilliant at everything.'

'All she's really good at is ordering people about,' I huffed, 'and moaning. Be dead funny though, Helena lying in state in the middle of a pile of cardboard and shredded tents.'

'That's not funny,' Trudie complained and then giggled. 'Magda would never live it down.'

'There she is,' I said. 'In the loading bay.'

'What took you so long?' Magda yelled as we crossed the tarmac. 'We have to be away from here by eight and we'll need *every* available minute.'

'What's up?' I asked, trying to maintain a suitable sombre expression and probably failing.

'It's too bloody *long*,' Magda snapped. 'We'll have to

cut about eighteen inches off or it won't go in the furnace.'

'What?' I'd heard what she said, but didn't believe it.

'The casket's too long,' she screeched. 'We have to shorten it and don't have much time. Come *on*.'

Magda disappeared, we scrambled to follow and found chaos inside the small side chapel where the dead waited their turn. The coffin rested on a wheeled gurney. One of the swooping ends had already been hacked off and was lying on the floor surrounded by pots of glue, saws and staplers. A tuft of multicoloured nylon peeped out through the hole and I was sure I could see Helena's feet, encased in a pair of sequined slippers. Spencer sat at a desk on one side of the room, fiddling with cables and computer equipment.

'Hi, Spencer,' I said. 'How's it going?'

'Cool,' he mumbled. 'Thought I'd check this out tonight – as you lot were going to be here anyway.'

'Emma!' Magda shouted. 'Stop chin-wagging and *help*. I can't do this on my own.'

I sighed: 'What do you want me to do?'

'I have to cut the baseboard,' Magda explained, picking up a panel saw, 'but Helena's legs are in the way. You and Trudie need to bend them up and hold them out of the way while I saw through the plank.'

I stared at her in disbelief. She looked very different from the floaty optimist I knew so well, I'll be honest, she looked deranged. Thick red hair had escaped from its band and dangled round her face, a mass of wild tangles. Her usually pale skin was flushed to an alarming shade of puce, a trickle of sweat slid down her nose and she waved the saw around dangerously.

73

'I'm not doing that!' Trudie protested. 'No way am I holding the legs of a dead woman.'

'You'll *have* to!' Magda said. 'No choice. If you don't help it'll be a *disaster.*'

'No, not a chance. Emma and Spencer can help if they want, but not me. I'm out.'

Trudie stalked away. I heard the outer door slam and knew she'd gone to wait in the car. I looked at Magda and thought she was going to cry. Her grand plan had disintegrated in fine style and for the first time ever, I felt genuinely sorry for her.

'Come on, Magda,' I said. 'It'll work out, don't worry. Spencer give us a hand.'

He hesitated before reluctantly leaving his computer equipment and shuffling over to the gurney.

'What do you want to me to do?' he mumbled.

'Help me push Helena's legs out of the way so Magda can cut the board off. It won't take long, will it, Magda?' I asked pointedly.

'No, not long, couple of minutes at the most.'

Gingerly I lifted Helena's feet and with Spencer's help, bent her legs, eased them further into the casket and exposed the baseboard. Magda dragged a chair next to the gurney, climbed on, bent over the plank and set to with the saw. As it turned out, the process didn't take a couple of minutes, it took much longer. The vibrations from the saw made it difficult to keep Helena's feet out of the way and the tent material frayed and tangled in the sharp teeth, slowing everything down. Magda rapidly lost any last remnants of cool she had and was soon using words I didn't realise she knew. I tried very hard not to laugh, but was gradually losing the battle. Control deserted me completely when one of the sequined slippers flew off Helena's foot and landed in the sawdust. Spencer let go of the legs to retrieve it and both feet shot out of the coffin like a horizontal jack-in-the-box. Magda stared in horror at the scene in front of her and while Spencer and I began to laugh, tears pouring down our faces, tears of misery poured down Magda's.

'Stop it! Stop it!' she screamed. 'Stop laughing, this isn't funny. It's a *catastrophe.*'

But much to her disappointment, we couldn't stop. I dusted sawdust off the slipper, shoved it back on Helena's foot and while Magda continued to sob, we opened the coffin lid, shifted the body so the feet finally vanished and closed the lid. Spencer wrenched the saw away from our distraught companion and quickly finished trimming the plank while I went in search of Trudie, who reluctantly returned to help us re-attach the end of the casket, paint in the missing wings on the new joint and clear up. We concealed our grins, spoke soothing words and rubbed Magda's back and slowly she returned to what passed for normal.

On our way home, we called in at a small pub and shared a couple of bottles of wine, we deserved a drink after the evening's exertions. We stayed until closing time and by the time we went our separate ways, Magda was once again in charge and calling the shots – and annoying me again. I'd be relieved when the cremation was over.

The chapel was packed. Everyone obeyed Magda's decree and dressed in rainbow colours, apart from one attendee who had dressed entirely in black, with a large brimmed hat. The waiting congregation was noisy and surprisingly gentle laughter rippled through the hubbub.

'I wish they'd quieten down,' Magda moaned. 'I *know* it's a celebration, but we have lost our friend, you'd think people would be a *bit* sad.'

'Honestly, Magda, you can't have it all,' I hissed at her. 'You can't control people's emotions, even if you think you can.'

Spencer appeared at my side: 'Emma, can I have a word?'

'What's wrong?' Magda snapped. 'Is there a problem with the streaming?'

'No, nothing's wrong,' he said. 'I just want a word with Emma, that's all.'

'Well make it quick, I'll be starting soon.' She marched off towards Trudie.

'What is it?' I asked. 'Is there a problem with the broadcast?'

'No, there really isn't, not *this* one anyway.'

'I'm not with you, you'll have to explain.'

Spencer swallowed: 'Magda must never find out,' he whispered.

'Find out what?'

'Last night, when we were messing ab . . . I mean, making the *adjustment,* well . . .' he ran out of steam.

'Bloody what? Spit it out will you?'

'OK, OK. Our session last night was captured by the webcam. I got involved in the DIY and . . . anyway, I didn't realise it was live, all of it is on the net. Magda mustn't find out, she'll do her nut.'

76

I watched as Magda in flowing, multicoloured robes, took her place at the lectern to begin the service. I studied the congregation and could tell from their faces that some had seen the impromptu webcast and those that hadn't, had been told about it. I chuckled as quietly as I could. Poor Magda, when she found out – and she would – she'd be *utterly appalled.*

TOURISTS DON'T KNOW WHERE THEY'VE BEEN

Sophie paused at the front of the tour bus, searching for an empty seat. Her eyes were drawn to a flapping pudgy hand, halfway back. Groaning inwardly she recognised Rachel, one half of the American couple she'd been stuck with at breakfast.

'Sophie! We've saved you a place.'

Sophie wound on a smile and trudged down the aisle to sit opposite the grinning couple, both loud, both overweight and dressed in matching jackets. The woman had big red hair tied with a clashing pink ribbon, her husband was almost bald.

'Told you she'd be on the tour, didn't I, Jim?'

Jim nodded.

'Thought you'd like some company,' Rachel nattered. 'Must be awful travelling alone – no one to talk to.'

'I don't mind, I'm used to it,' Sophie mumbled.

'Ain't that a shame? Pretty girl like you shouldn't be alone.'

The driver climbed the stairs and settled behind the wheel as a tour guide began a head count, waving a gold pen in the air as though she was conducting an orchestra. The engine grumbled into life and the coach pulled away from the hotel.

'We've an hour's drive,' Jim announced, studying a brochure. 'Through 'verdant countryside' it says here.'

Sophie gazed through the glass, marvelled at the incredible light, vivid colours and a hundred shades of green. Dense undergrowth crowded each side of the potholed tarmac and tyres rumbled over the rough surface. The sun was hot and her sweating body stuck to uncomfortable plastic seats.

'Been looking forward to this trip, haven't we, Jim?' Rachel gushed. 'Heard the place was going to open to tourists soon after it closed and put our names down. Didn't think we'd be on the inaugural trip though.'

Sophie nodded and wished the woman would stop talking – just for a while – but there was no respite. At least Rachel didn't leave any gaps in the stream of words spilling from her mouth, so Sophie didn't have to think of anything to say.

Rachel dug in her voluminous handbag and dragged out a bag of sweets: 'Help yourself, dear, stop your mouth going dry. Can't drink too much on a coach tour, don't always know when the next bathroom opportunity will come along.'

Sophie declined and curled her mouth into a passable smile, the task more difficult each time. She looked back out the window as the coach passed a settlement of colourful houses with brightly painted doors, ancient cars parked by the kerb, chickens pecking in the dust, scabby cats lounging on crumbling brick walls.

'We've done a heap of travelling since Jim retired, haven't we, Jim? Been all over the world. Where did you say you were from, dear?'

'Birmingham, England.'

'Our first vacation was to the UK. London, Stratford-upon-Avon – all the sights, but we didn't make it to Birming-ham.'

Sophie caught Jim's eye and wondered how he put up with his wife's constant monologue, sure she'd be insane within a week.

'I wonder what it will be like,' Rachel babbled. 'There aren't many photos in the leaflet and none of the inside, bit different from our previous trips. We went to 'The Rock' last year, didn't we, Jim?'

Jim nodded.

'You know, Sophie – Alcatraz – stunning. Definitely my favourite, twenty-two acres of heaven if you ask me. I said to Jim, if I ever had to go to jail, Alcatraz would be the place, floating in the sea just off San Francisco. The warden's house is still standing, must have been a grand place. Shame the Indians torched the place during their occupation in '69. Destruction for destruction's sake if you ask me. Amazing thing; the guides were all ex-prisoners, really old men, but it's good they have employment.'

Rachel paused for breath and Jim snatched the opportunity to get a word in.

'Weren't keen on Auschwitz, nasty atmosphere.' Jim took a bite of an overstuffed sandwich, mumbling round the food clogging his mouth. Sophie's nostrils cringed as she smelt egg. 'Flat with big skies,' he continued, 'they dropped us *miles* away from the entrance and expected us to *walk* along the railroad track. Couldn't see the point of that at all. One of the cheapest tours though, tickets came free with the hotel room and we got twenty percent off for booking early.'

Rachel butted in: 'No birds, didn't see a single critter all the time we were there. Personally, I found the place very haunting, but then,' she leant forward in her seat and whispered the last three words as though she was in church; 'I'm a survivor.'

'You're not old enough?' Sophie spluttered, eyebrows raised.

'I wasn't *there*, silly,' Rachel giggled. 'My grandfather murdered in the camp, so all my family are survivors. Mother escaped to the States early on in the war.'

Sophie felt her eyes widen and hoped Rachel hadn't noticed. She wondered what was wrong with the woman and took a long drink from a plastic water bottle. Even before noon the island was hot, especially inland. The coast occasionally provided a sea breeze, but even the wind was hot. She peered through the window and saw less in the way of vegetation and more dust. The further North-West the bus travelled, the wider and better surfaced the road became. She glanced at her watch and tried to work out how much longer she'd be stuck with the awful Americans.

'Robben Island was OK, but not much there,' Jim said, swigging from a coke can to wash down the sandwich. 'No point in going back once you've been. Took a photo of Rachel standing in Nelson Mandela's *actual* cell, and we saw the lime works where men sentenced to hard labour were sent. Ex-prisoners working as guides there too, shame they were so difficult to understand – they all mumbled.'

Rachel couldn't keep quiet: 'Amazing gift shop and restaurant, we had lunch there, didn't we, Jim?'

Jim nodded and sank his teeth into another sandwich. A blob of mayonnaise squirted down his chin and Sophie looked away.

'Should be nearly there now,' Rachel said, leaning into the aisle, trying to peer through the windscreen. 'Can't see anything, just acres of weeds and dust. Isn't the sea somewhere near? I could do with stretching my legs.'

The woman prattled away and at last, Sophie managed to filter out the irritating drone and sink into her own thoughts. She hadn't wanted to come here, but when she received the pass in the post felt that *someone* should. Now she was actually here, stuck with these dreadful people, on a bus full of other dreadful people, she considered her decision nuts. She should have stayed away, there was nothing for her here.

The tour guide addressed the passengers using a microphone and when Rachel piped up again, Sophie imagined slapping the woman into silence and sat on her hands in case she was tempted. She shouldn't have come. She never wanted to be here.

When the pass had arrived at her family home in Birmingham she hid the envelope for a week, unsure what to do with it. Eventually, she rang her uncle and offered him the pass. He didn't want it – considered himself too old to make the trip – but said Sophie should go. It was his opinion if she turned down the opportunity she might regret it later, so here she was – on the bus.

Opening her bag, she dug around until she found a tatty envelope and checked its contents. The pass was still there and Sophie slipped it out.

Rachel peered over Sophie's shoulder: 'What's that?'

she asked. 'Looks like a Triple A pass, access all areas. Do you work there?'

Sophie shook her head and wished she'd had the sense to leave the wretched thing in her bag, thus avoiding the inevitable inquisition.

The bus braked, jolted to a stop and the tour guide began issuing instructions. Passengers chattered excitedly, hauled themselves to their feet and searched for bags in overhead racks. A man in military uniform climbed the stairs of the bus and unhooked the microphone.

'Good morning, everyone. All passengers please remain seated. Is Miss Sophie Malik present?'

Sophie raised her hand hesitantly, aware that the Americans were staring at her.

'If you'd follow me, ma'am,' the officer said.

Sophie stood and as she began to move Rachel grabbed her hand and tugged insistently, annoyingly.

'How come you're getting a private tour, are you an inspector or something? Last minute checks?'

Sophie turned and glared at Rachel: 'No, I'm not an inspector, or a tour guide, or a worker in the bound to be well-appointed gift shop or café. My father was imprisoned here for ten years, kidnapped at a family wedding in Pakistan by bounty hunters who sold him to *your* government for $5000. There was never a charge levelled against him, he wasn't allowed visitors, or legal representation or even letters – if the authorities didn't think he'd earned them.' Words tumbled from her mouth. She felt her skin flush and made an effort to stop speaking.

Rachel was silent – for a heartbeat – then asked: 'Where is your father now, dear, with the place being closed, did they send him home?'

'No, they didn't, they sent home his body, told us he'd killed himself, but I don't believe that, neither do the rest of the family.'

'Miss Malik?' the officer called.

Sophie yanked her hand away, aware that every pair of eyes in the bus was on her. She lifted her head, regained her composure, walked down the aisle, stepped out of the bus and stood on the dust.

All she could see was wire; coiled wire, razor wire, barbed wire, wire tunnels and cages that glinted wickedly in the bright sunlight. Taking a deep breath she fell in step beside the officer as he strode towards the main gate of Camp X-ray, Guantanamo, Cuba, now open to tourists for a $50 entrance fee.

(NB: the comments made by the American couple are genuine reviews discovered on the internet)

THE LAST WORD

The parcel was waiting for me when I arrived home from work, propped against the front door – odd – I hadn't ordered anything, but maybe Mark had. I plonked it on the kitchen table and poured myself a much needed glass of wine, before examining the delivery.

It was about the size of a dress box, wrapped in brown paper and wasn't very heavy. An envelope addressed to me, was glued to the front. Peeling it away I discovered it contained a letter from a firm of solicitors in South Wales.

'Dear Ms Stanhope,

We are very sorry to inform you of the recent death of your ex-husband, Andrew Brennan.'

Almost instantly – and unexpectedly – I experienced a jolt of pain for the death of a long ago lover. Wiping my face, I poured more wine and read the rest of the letter.

'Andrew died at home after a short illness. He mentioned you in his will and, as executors, we now send you his bequest.

Would you please acknowledge receipt . . .'

Putting the letter aside I ripped open the brown paper, unable to imagine what Andrew might have left me. We divorced nearly twelve years ago and I couldn't actually remember the last time I'd thought about him. The split had been extremely acrimonious. Money had always been an issue between us and after the divorce, I took on the mortgage and kept the house. Andrew had been furious and we hadn't spoken since, but maybe he'd forgiven me, hence the bequest.

I tugged off the paper and uncovered a fancy box with an indigo blue lid, edged in gold and tied with a satin ribbon. A tiny envelope was tucked under the knot and inside was a business card: *'Fiore Leathers Ltd.'* Intrigued, I was about to remove the lid, when I heard Mark's key in the front door.

'Ilsa,' he called. 'You home?'

'Kitchen,' I shouted and poured him a glass of wine.

He slouched in, planted a token kiss on my cheek – a wasted gesture in a wasted relationship – and greedily slurped his drink.

'What's that?' he asked and nodded at the box.

I pushed the solicitor's letter towards him and watched as he read.

'That's a bit of a shocker,' he said. 'Did you know your ex had shuffled off?'

I shook my head: 'Haven't heard from him since the divorce, haven't *thought* about him in years. He was only a couple of years older than me; I wonder what he died of?'

'What did he leave you? A bundle of crisp, twenty-pound notes would be handy.'

'Where would Andrew have got that sort of money?

'He might have won the lottery for all you know. Open the box and find out.'

I tucked my fingers under the lid and eased out the bottom; air sucked at the cardboard. Inside was a thick layer of blue tissue paper and I carefully unfolded it while

87

Mark stood in the doorway watching.

'If he's sent you underwear I'm gonna be pissed off,' he grumbled.

'Why on *earth* would a dead man send me underwear?' His unreasonable jealousy irritated me.

I removed the last sheet of tissue and my eyes were assaulted by colours so bright it looked as though the box was lit from within.

'What *is* that?' Mark asked. 'A shawl?'

I gently rubbed one edge of the fabric between my fingers. It was as soft as chamois leather or fine silk, reminded me of something and a distant memory nudged my brain. Mark reached into the box, snatched at the contents and I stopped him.

'Don't!'

'I can't see what it is,' he grumbled. 'Let me pull it out.'

'I *know* what it is.' I poured another glass of wine.

'So, what is it?'

'Andrew's tattoos . . . his skin.'

Mark burst out laughing, but stopped abruptly when I didn't join in and stared at me.

'You're kidding aren't you?' he asked. 'Never mind *why* he left you his skin, *how* would he? Do undertakers offer flaying these days?'

'I don't know!' I snapped. 'But that's definitely his skin. I recognise the koi carp, I paid for it as a birthday present the second year we were together.'

'Why the *hell* would he send you his skin? That's just gross.'

'When the tattoo was finished, I joked he should leave

me his skin as the work was so expensive and far too beautiful for cremation or burial. I wasn't *serious.'*

'Well, Andrew thought you were – obviously. Bloody disgusting if you ask me, you should chuck it away.'

'I can't do that,' I objected, 'it wouldn't be right.'

'What wouldn't be right about it?'

'Doesn't feel right, anyway, dumping bits of dead people in wheelie bins is bound to be illegal.'

We fell silent and stared at the tattoos. The koi was so vivid and lifelike, as though it was swimming in a dark pool. A pink lotus flower completed the illusion. I stretched out my hand and brushed the jet and vermillion scales with my fingertips.

'Don't touch the bloody thing,' Mark protested and smacked my hand away.

'Why not? It's been tanned, feels like soft suede.' I pushed the box towards him and he recoiled violently.

'Get rid of it! What did that twisted bastard expect you to do with it, pin it on the wall, lampshades perhaps?'

'Shut up, Mark, that's sick.'

'And sending someone your skin isn't?' He made a grab for the box and I slid it out of his reach.

'Give it here,' he ordered. 'You're not keeping it.'

'Don't tell me what I can and can't do,' I retaliated, for once not allowing him to bully me.

'This is ridiculous! I'm going out and *that thing* needs to be gone by the time I get back.'

'Or what?' I taunted.

He shot me one of his disgusted looks and stormed out.

This was how things had been for a while now and I

was sick of it. Mark had become increasingly short-tempered and dictatorial and arguments blew up from nowhere.

I reached into the box, lifted out the hide gently and spread it on the table. There were three sections, two were obviously shoulder-chest-arm pieces, I could tell by the shape, the third was a long wide strip, maybe from the spine. I sniffed it tentatively, but all I could smell was leather, like the seats in my father's old car – comforting.

The tattoos were astonishing. The carp and lotus were joined by mystical symbols, jungle undergrowth, twisted vines, more flowers, humming birds and Chinese hanzi. I discovered a miniature bumble-bee in the centre of one of the flowers, a hovering emerald dragonfly and a crimson ladybird. The skin was beautiful, a work of art and I knew I'd never be able to throw it away.

I held a section up to the light and the tattoos became a stained glass window . . . maybe blinds, but would it fade? Lampshades were out of the question. Perhaps I could get it mounted in a frame and hang it on the wall, not that Mark would allow that. I draped a piece over my shoulder, it hung down my arm and felt – nice. I went into the hall so I could look in the full-length mirror and wondered if it was possible to incorporate the panels in something to wear, and if it was, would – or should – I wear it?

I recalled the day the carp had been inked onto Andrew's skin, a happy day. I missed happy days and now I thought about it, missed Andrew too. Was that because he was dead, or had I always missed him? I was so immersed in my thoughts I didn't hear Mark open the door.

'What the bloody hell do you think you're doing?' he yelled and tried to wrench the skin away. I ducked back into the kitchen and stashed my treasure safely in the box.

'I'm not staying here with that thing,' he said.

'Fine, go then!' I shouted. 'I'm fed up with you telling me what to do and how to think. This has nothing to do with you, so shut up, or get out.'

He looked shocked and I knew I'd called his bluff. Not wanting to look like a loser, he shouted some more and stormed upstairs, hurling down the odd obscenity, before stomping out with a large backpack and a suitcase.

The silence he left behind was welcoming; I actually breathed a sigh of relief. I'd been trying to get rid of him for months now, but hadn't been able to devise a way to break the news. This ending had been so unforeseen – and so easy.

On Saturday I went to visit my favourite dressmaker, Pav, to show him the leather, hoping he'd have some ideas. He lived not far from me with his husband – Bruce – and I decided to walk. I relished the novelty of making my own choices and not having to be in on time or lie about where I was going. Macho-Mark, as they called him, heartily disapproved of my friends.

Bruce made coffee while Pav spread the leather sections on his cutting table.

'Wow,' was all he said and held a finger to pursed lips. 'Wow!'

'Like it?' I asked.

'I love it. Exquisite! The quality of the tanning is some of the best I've ever seen.'

'Can you do anything with it?'

Bruce appeared with coffee and Pav flapped him away.

'Don't you *dare* come any closer until your hands are empty and when they are, take a look at what Ilsa's brought.'

We all bent over the table and discovered tiny details tucked away in the mass of ink.

'Where did you get this, honey?' Pav asked, peering at me over the top of orange framed glasses.

'Ah . . .' I hesitated. 'Now, that's the thing.'

'What's the *thing*?'

'Do you remember Andrew Brennan?' I asked. 'I was married to him in previous life.'

'I remember.' Pav giggled, 'such a shame he batted for your side, he was *gorgeous*.'

'Well, he died and left me this.' I pointed at the table, 'his tattoos . . . his skin.'

'Human leather!' Pav squeaked. 'How exciting to have the chance to work with something so special. It screams, "short-suede-jacket" to me, with the panels worked in against a black background. Bit of luck, the strip of hanzis should make a wide belt. What do you think?'

His response wasn't what I had been expecting, but I was delighted he'd agreed to take the job on. He buzzed around with a tape measure and made some rough sketches before promising he'd have something to show me in a couple of weeks.

'Come round for dinner,' I said. 'I'll cook. It's ages

since we've got together.'

'Won't Macho-Mark have something to say about that?' Bruce asked.

'He might, but we've spilt. He left Wednesday and I haven't had any messages, so I guess that's it. All over.'

Pav bounced up and down on his toes and clapped his hands.

'Well done, girl! He wasn't right for you, nasty bully, never did like him. Dinner will be fab. I'll phone when the jacket is ready.'

'Great. Can either of you get the Chinese characters translated, it'll be good to know what it says; might read 'sweet and sour chicken'.'

Bruce chuckled, 'I'll ask at the tattoo parlour and if they don't know, I've got a mate at the club who might.'

A couple of weeks later Pav and Bruce arrived on my doorstep bringing the jacket with them and as I slipped it on, the soft leather brushed my cheek like a lover's caress. *Andrew*? The design had brought the art to life and as I moved my arms and watched the fish dance across my shoulder. I stroked the scales, entranced.

'You don't want to do too much of that,' Pav scolded me. 'It'll pick up the grease.' He tweaked the collar and gently tugged on the sleeves. 'Like it?'

'It's extraordinary! I adore it, talk about *haute couture.*'

Pav giggled: 'No one else is going to have one, that's for sure. An absolute one-off, just like you.'

'Any luck with the belt?' I asked.

Bruce handed over a bundle and watched as I

unrolled it. It reminded me of a snake's skin and as I wrapped it around my waist it seemed to constrict gently – like a one-handed hug.

'Did you manage to find someone to translate the hanzis?' I asked.

Bruce nodded.

'Tell me then, what does it say?'

'Was Andrew a bit of a joker?' he asked.

'Sometimes, why?'

Bruce appeared reluctant to answer but eventually said; 'I guess a literal translation would be – "You had the shirt".'

CHAD WOZ 'ERE

No one was entirely sure when the graffiti appeared on the back of the newly refurbished village hall. Lizzie Evans first spotted it on Bank Holiday Monday during her return journey through the meadow after walking her dog, Charlie. The mural depicted an enormous white elephant blowing bank notes from its trunk, and covered the entire back wall of the hall – or 'Village Shed' – as residents who weren't committee members referred to it.

Lizzie stood in the field, knee deep in meadowsweet and red champion, and stared in disbelief while her smoke-grey lurcher lolloped around in the long grass, chasing butterflies and grasshoppers.

'Hey, Charlie,' she shouted. 'Look at the picture.'

The dog briefly raised his head, saw nothing to interest him and began hunting mice in the dense bramble patches. Lizzie called him to her side, slipped on the lead and headed back through the small village, looking forward to coffee. A slightly bent figure was walking along the pavement and she recognised Dai, an elderly man who had lived in the village since he was born in his parent's bedroom at number six, nearly eighty years ago.

'Morning, Lizzie,' he called, a broad smile on his face. 'How are you today?'

'Good thanks.' She walked closer and murmured in his ear: 'Have you seen the elephant on the back of the Village

Shed?'

Dai chuckled: 'Yeah, saw it yesterday, it's bloody marvellous don't you think?'

'I do – but the committee won't like it – not one little bit.'

'Of course they won't, too close to the knuckle after they spent over a hundred thousand on a place no one uses, way too much for a glorified shed. I still can't work out how they got the grants.'

'Nor me – not in these days of austerity. Any idea who painted it?'

Dai shrugged: 'I wonder how long it will be before the committee see it?'

'Probably a while, I've never seen any of them walking in the meadow and I'm not going to tell them, they'll only want to get rid of it. I think it's lovely and so clever, all those floating tenners. Shame it isn't on the front so everyone passing by can see it.'

A week later when the artwork had finally been noticed by the universally detested Village Hall Committee, an emergency public meeting was called and – unusually – a smattering of residents turned out on a wet night to discover what would be done. The four officials sat at the head of the table, while villagers chatted amongst themselves and waited for the chairperson – a woman with an unattractive nature called June – to open the meeting. She eventually rapped loudly on the table with her knuckles and gazed around the room at the unexpectedly large turnout.

'Good evening,' she said, with a smile that didn't reach her eyes. 'Nice to see so many of you here. As you know, we have called you together to discuss the vandalism to the back of the hall. This is a serious matter – criminal damage – although the police don't seem very interested.' She scrutinized her audience hoping for support, but no one spoke. 'Anyway,' she continued, 'does anyone know anything about this, like when it was carried out or who was responsible?'

Lizzie Evans lifted a tentative hand: 'It appeared over the bank holiday weekend. I saw it first when Charlie and I came through the field after our walk.' She hesitated: 'I have to say I think it's rather good.'

'Rather good!' June screeched. 'It's not at all good, dreadful white scribble, a desecration. It cost a fortune to have the walls painted and treated after the refurbishment and it will all have to be redone and that means more expense.' An indignant red flush coloured her cheeks.

'You're not planning to paint over it are you?' Lizzie asked.

'Of course. What else would we do?'

'Well . . . keep it. Other villages and towns locally have murals and now we have one.'

'No, no, no,' June said. 'It must be painted over.'

'I don't see why,' Donald from number eight said. 'I like it too.' His amusement was barely concealed: 'Is it because you object to the subject matter? I mean, a white elephant? Rather prescient don't you think.' He grinned. 'And I'm not sure a village hall can be desecrated, being it's not a sacred or holy place.'

Mumbled assent rumbled around the room, interspersed with a few quiet giggles and June's skin

98

flushed again.

'That's not very helpful,' she said. 'What we should be doing is devising a plan to raise the money we'll need to put things right.'

'We should take a vote,' Dai muttered from the end of the table.

'A vote?' June spluttered. 'What the hell for?'

'To decide whether the village wants to keep the mural.'

June frowned: 'It's fairly obvious we don't.'

Dai shook his head: 'It's obvious *you* don't, but the village shed is owned by all of us so we should have a say, anyway – it could be a Banksy for all we know.'

June opened her mouth to say something but as Dai's words finally reached her grey matter, anything she had been planning to say never left her mouth.

'Wow,' Donald said. 'Do you think that's possible, Dai?'

'Looks like a lot of his other stuff to me but I'm no expert.'

'How much would it be worth?'

Dai rubbed his stubbly chin with grubby fingers: 'Difficult to say but the last time one was sold it went for £300k.'

'How much?' June spluttered, suddenly interested again now that money had been mentioned – and so much of it.

'I heard about that,' Lizzie said. 'It was on a garage in Port Talbot and much smaller than our elephant.'

The retired colonel suddenly came to life, thick eyebrows bouncing: 'That certainly puts a very different light on things.'

'Doesn't it,' Dai said. 'If there's the chance it *is* a

Banksy we'll need to protect it. A 24 hour watch should be arranged.'

June huffed and shook her head: 'That's ridiculous, it's not going anywhere.'

'But it *could*,' Donald said. 'The building is wooden. I imagine the back wall could be sliced off fairly easily and if that happens, you'll need a lot more money for repairs.'

'He's right,' Lizzie said. 'I heard on the radio that Banksies are always getting stolen. It's precious and we should look after it.'

June reluctantly agreed and informed the meeting she would speak with the local police to arrange protection of the mural.

Dai laughed: 'They won't do that – not without us paying them. They aren't security guards. We'll have to take care of the thing ourselves until we can get someone to take a look.'

'How long will that take?' June asked. 'And who would we ask?'

Donald cleared his throat: 'Steven – my life-partner,' he said, as though no one knew, 'owns a gallery in Bristol – Banksy's home town – and I'm sure he'd be able to confirm the artwork's authenticity – or not. He's away until next week though – Newport on a buying trip.'

'Couldn't he nip back?' June asked. 'This is a fairly urgent matter.'

Donald smiled: 'Newport, Rhode Island – America.'

Dai raised a wrinkly hand: 'I've got an old touring caravan,' he said. 'We could tow it to the back of the shed, stick a couple of residents inside and they can act as round-the-clock security.'

The overweight treasurer, who rarely spoke out loud, leaned closer to June and whispered in her ear. The meeting held its collective breath and watched as June bobbed her head like a nodding dog on the dashboard of a Ford Escort. Eventually the confab came to an end.

'OK,' June said. 'This is what we'll do. We'll use Dai's caravan and volunteers can man it until Steven returns from America. Next week you said, Donald?'

Donald nodded: 'Back on Friday.'

'That's six days away!'

Donald nodded again.

June sighed: 'Then we'll need as many volunteers as possible.'

Dai raised his hand once more: 'I don't think that's a good idea. With something as valuable as a Banksy, it should be committee members who take responsibility, and as you're also trustees, you effectively own the place on behalf of the residents.'

'Here, here,' The Colonel said, followed by: 'Quite right.' Then folded his arms across his considerable belly and closed his eyes.

The committee officials huddled together like a rugby scrum in miniature and mumbled conspiratorially. Eventually June restarted proceedings with a sharp knock on the table, even though the room was already quiet.

'Dai is right,' June announced, 'and the committee agree. We will guard the hall until Steven gets home. When can you move your caravan, Dai?'

'I'll need an hour or so but you'll be able to use it tonight. Wrap up warm though and bring a thermos, the gas is out so no heating or boiling kettles.'

The day before Steven returned from The States, Lizzie was out walking Charlie. The weather had turned colder at the start of the week, a late frost had coated the mountain during the night and shallow puddles in the car park at the rear of the hall were filmy with ice. As the pair wandered past the tatty caravan, the door opened and June stepped out. She was heavily bundled in coats and scarves, a fleecy blanket around her shoulders and was obviously in a hurry to unlock the hall so she could avail herself of the facilities. She looked frozen, eyes redrimmed from lack of sleep, not dissimilar to a homeless person. She nodded brusquely at Lizzie and scuttled away. Lizzie paused to gaze at the elephant, smile at the fountain of tenners spewing from its trunk and admire the skill and nerve required to create the piece. Hearing a noise to her left she glanced over her shoulder and saw Dai walking towards her from the direction of the field.

'Morning, Lizzie.'

'Morning, Dai,' she answered. 'Have you come to look at Claude?'

'Who?'

'Our white elephant, I've named him Claude.'

Dai chuckled.

'If he's real,' Lizzie continued, 'do you think the committee will let us keep him or will they sell him?'

'Bound to sell him, yet more money to waste on a glorified wooden shed no one wants.'

'Such a shame. I've become quite attached and will miss him if he's taken away. I had entertained the idea of opening an arts centre, Claude would be ideal as our centre piece. How much do you think he's worth?'

Dai shrugged: 'Dunno, 50p maybe.'

Lizzie laughed: 'They'll get much more than that and sadly I think you're right, as soon as Steven confirms the work is a genuine Banksy, they'll flog it to the highest bidder.'

'He won't though, will he?' Dai muttered.

'Why won't he?' Lizzie asked.

'Cos it's not real, it isn't a Banksy.' Dai opened his coat and allowed Lizzie to see several empty cans of white aerosol paint. 'I've been getting rid of evidence,' he whispered.

Lizzie's eyes opened wide and she squeaked: '*You* did it? Why?'

Dai smiled: 'Why not? It's what we all think, and maybe a few days out here cooling their heels will put a halt to the rubbishy hot air the committee talk. And of course, as it isn't real, maybe they will let us keep it. We didn't get to vote on Claude's future at the last meeting, so I'll make sure hold a ballot before any painting over business goes on. They're bound to be outnumbered.'

Lizzie giggled: 'I hope so, but guess I should probably change his name to Fraud.'

Dai grinned: 'Call it anything you like as long as you don't call it a Daisky.'

DOCTOR KNOWS BEST

Whichever way I look at things I'm in deep shit; credit cards maxed out, mortgage due and the overdraft has topped £2,000. I spread the paperwork on the desk and the debts singe my eyes. This collection doesn't even include substantial costs generated by my high-maintenance mistress, the cost of keeping two ungrateful brats at public school and a wife with no understanding of money.

A tap on the door startled me. I gathered the bills into a heap and stuffed them in a drawer as Val stuck her head in.

'Doctor, Susan Pearce is in the waiting room,' she said. 'Her GP isn't in today and she's had a fall. Will you see her?'

'Of course, send her in.'

Susan hobbled in leaning heavily on a stick. She was short and dumpy, dull blonde hair scraped into a pony-tail, skin the colour of overcooked pasta.

'Hiya, Doc,' she said. 'I fell yesterday, but everyfin' 'urts worse today. Me ankle's swolled – can't put any weight on it – ricked me thumb an' all.'

She dumped her handbag on the floor, mobile on my desk.

I pulled over a stool. 'Let's take a look, put your foot up.'

She grunted in pain and peeling off a sticky pink

sock, I was confronted by a multicoloured ankle. I probed and Susan winced.

'Steady, Doc. Fell over a paving stone, well, where a stone *should* have been. Look at me thumb.'

She shoved the digit under my nose.

'Bloody council shouldn't leave 'oles for people to fall in. What d'you reckon, 'ave I broke anyfin?'

'Can you wiggle your toes?'

Susan pulled a face, concentrated on her foot and reassuringly did have limited movement.

'I'm sure it's a sprain,' I said, 'with probable ligament damage. I'll send you for an x-ray to be sure. Now, show me your hand.'

I gently took hold of her wrist to manipulate the thumb joint. She yelped.

'Where did you fall?' I asked.

'Middle of the estate, looks like someone's nicked a slab. I reported it last month, but the bloody council are bloody useless.'

'Well, it doesn't look as though you've broken any bones, but we'll have your thumb checked at the same time as your ankle. I hope you're going to make a claim.'

'A claim?'

'To the council. You'd have a good case, especially if you can prove you reported the hole. Was there anything to warn pedestrians?'

'Nuffin', just the bloody 'ole. I was out shoppin' with me sister. She brought me here today; said I should get checked.'

'Quite right and if you *do* make a claim, you'll need medical reports.'

''Ow much d'you reckon I'd get?'

'Depends on the damage. Soft tissue injuries don't pay anything like as much as fractures.' I consulted the internet. 'For example, a Rolando fracture – broken thumb – usually needs surgery; average payout £36,000.'

''Ow much?' she spluttered.

'A broken talus – the bone on the top of your foot – might pay £12,000.' I paused, watching as she struggled with the mental arithmetic.

'That's nearly fifty grand!' she exclaimed.

'But – as I said – I don't think you've broken any bones.'

'I'll get somefin' though, won't I? For the pain and sufferin'.'

'Maybe. It'll take time to make a claim, but you might end up with a couple of thousand.'

Her face fell.

'What's wrong?' I asked.

'That ain't enough,' she said. 'Got meself in trouble, 'ad a bad patch with the kids – borrowed money from this bloke. Fings didn't get better, so I borrowed more, then started missin' payments. I owe *so* much I don't fink I'll get clear before I die – and I ain't fifty yet.' Tears began to flow and I handed her a tissue box.

'Daft ain't it,' she sniffed. 'I should be *grateful* I ain't broke nuffin', but it would be dead handy if I 'ad. Clear me loans and change.'

I hesitated before I spoke: 'There *is* a way I could help.'

''Ow? Write a letter saying I broke me bones?'

'Can't do that, x-rays will prove otherwise.'

106

'Wot then?'

I weighed up the situation. I've always been a good judge of people – needed to be – what I was about to suggest went against *every* rule in *every* book.

'When you're examined at hospital they'll expect fractures,' I said.

The next part was tricky. Some patients were grateful for my help, some weren't and I always ran the risk of being reported. It's difficult to admit, but I think the *risk-excitement* is one of the reasons I do what I do.

'If you agree, I can anesthetise your thumb and ankle, give the respective bones a bit of a tap, then x-rays will show fractures required to claim compensation.'

'Will it 'urt?' she asked.

'You'll feel something, but the aesthetic will keep pain to a minimum.'

'You said, 'bit of a tap', what *exactly* does that mean?'

'I'll place a small block on the bones and give them a swift whack. A spilt second.'

''Ave you done it before?'

'A couple of times,' I lied. I'd done this more times than I could count. How else had I managed to live so far beyond my means?

'Does it always work?' Susan asked.

'Never had a claim rejected,' I boasted.

''Ow much do *you* want?'

'Forty percent, same as no-win-no-fee lawyers.'

'Sounds like a lot to me, that means you'd get . . . ah . . .'

'If you're awarded £48,000, you'll keep £28,800. My fee will *only* be £19,200.'

'Bloody hell, that's a lot of dosh for a 'couple of taps'.'

'I'm running a huge risk and you're buying my expertise. I know *where* to tap and *how* hard and guarantee you won't be left with any long term problems. You'll be in plaster anyway because of the ligament damage, so why not? The payout would solve your money problems.'

'Yeah, it would, but are you sure it won't 'urt?'

'It'll happen so fast you'll hardly be aware of it and – I promise you – I know what I'm doing.'

I watched her thinking. Her eyelids crinkled, nostrils flared and she rubbed her forehead as though trying to jump-start her brain.

'Can I fink about it?'

'We *really* need to do it as soon as possible. I can do it now, call an ambulance and they'll take you straight to hospital.'

'Bones take longer to heal than ligaments don't they? And it'll 'urt a lot more won't it?'

'Probably not and they'll give you strong painkillers at hospital. I know what I'm doing and ridding yourself of debt can only improve your health in the long term. You might be able to stop taking antidepressants.'

I saw her reach a decision: 'Yeah, alright then, do it, before I change me mind.'

I tackled the thumb first and flooded the area with aesthetic before strapping her hand to the desk, trapezoid joint uppermost. I held a wooden block on the bone, a surgical hammer in the other.

'On three,' I said, but brought the hammer down on one. She jumped and reflexively tried to pull her hand away, but felt little extra pain.

'Perfect!' I said. 'Are you OK?'

'I guess,' she said, 'but get on wiv it, I want it over.'

The second procedure was much the same. I strapped her ankle in position, more aesthetic and a bigger block that spanned the talus bone. I didn't count this time, just whacked the wood as hard as I could and felt the bone beneath give. Susan felt the blow and briefly lost consciousness. I untied her leg and called an ambulance.

As she was loaded in the back, I passed over her mobile phone and handbag and told her I'd visit in a couple of weeks, but if she needed anything in the meantime to call me.

Two weeks later I made the promised house-call. I didn't like driving into the estate, a desperately deprived area with a shocking reputation, but it was considered safe during daylight hours. Susan lived in a pokey flat on the fifth floor of a tower block, with two small boys and her sister. Sally was a thinner, older version of Susan, with a pinched, angular face, short greasy hair and tattoos covered her arms.

'Sit down, Doc,' Susan said. There was no offer of tea.

'How are you?' I asked. 'Managing the plaster-casts OK? Pain controlled?'

'Yeah, all's fine, ta.'

'And how are things going with the claim?'

'Slow. You were right, it'll take a while before I get any dosh, but the loan shark's backed off.'

'That's good news. You'll let me know when the cheque arrives won't you?' I asked pointedly.

Sally spoke for the first time: 'Why would Susan let *you* know?'

'Well . . .' I didn't like the way she looked at me. 'We have an agreement.'

'Wotever *agreement* you 'ad is broke,' Sally growled, 'just like me sister's bones. You ain't getting nuthin'. Pay you for mutilating people? As if!'

'Hang on, I freed Susan from her money worries, and we made an *agreement*.'

'We're gonna make a new one.' Sally fiddled with her phone and I heard my voice float out of a tiny speaker: '. . . I can anesthetise your thumb and ankle, give the respective bones a bit of a tap . . .'

'You recorded me?' I stammered and glared at Susan.

'Damn right! We 'eard what you been up to, that's why Sis brought me to you.'

Sally tapped more buttons and I heard myself say: 'place a small block on the bone we want to break and give it a swift whack.'

'Stop,' I begged. 'You don't want to pay commission, that's fine as long as you give me that recording.'

'Bloody *obvious* you won't be gettin' anyfin',' Susan said, 'but that ain't all. We want 'alf of any future *earnings* and if we don't get it, we'll give this to the cops.'

'*What?* That's impossible. I can't afford that.'

'When GP's are earnin' 140 grand?' Sally snapped. 'That's wot the Daily Mail says and you got all that *extra* dosh rollin' in. You'll find a way to pay, you *know* you will, or you'll get sacked and end up livin' somewhere like this. You'll love that,' she sneered.

'Can I have time to think about it?' I asked, voice

110

unsteady.

'Like you gave *me* time to fink before you smashed me bones?' Susan asked.

I felt sweat on my back, collar stuck unpleasantly to my neck. I loosened my tie: 'Don't have a choice do I?'

'No,' Susan chuckled, 'and if you don't pay, Sally knows some lads who'll enjoy collectin' what you owe.'

I felt ill and needed to leave. I grabbed my bag, stumbled through the door onto the concrete walkway, sure I was having a panic attack; unable to breathe. I rested my bag on the balcony wall and sat next to it, feeling light-headed. I couldn't believe *everything* in my life was shattering so easily, that a couple of women from a place like *this* could get the better of me when I was trying to help. I stared at the front door, willed it to open and the sisters to say they were joking, but it stayed shut.

Feeling the breeze on my face I stared across the city; great view, but I couldn't live in a place like this. I smelt greasy cooking, urine, cannabis and dirt; heard screaming babies, fighting teenagers, loud music, domestic arguments and *knew* I couldn't live here, or find enough cash to pay the evil sisters.

I grabbed my bag and set off down the stairs. Rounding a corner I swung on a metal banister and felt it give under my weight, screws ripped from the concrete and rattled away. I lost my footing and tumbled, ricocheted off a wall and plummeted another flight. Something crunched in my chest, a sharp pain in my thigh made me cry out and I thought Susan was right – the bloody council *were* bloody useless.

PENNY'S FROM HELL

Wednesday's were Jim's least favourite day of the week. On Wednesdays his daughter, Penny called in. Her mother, his wife, died nearly four years ago and he missed his gentle Gwen. It seemed she had been the only one who could control Penny and the longer Gwen had been gone, the more egregious his daughter had become. She visited out of a sense of duty and didn't try to pretend otherwise.

The first week of February, Penny was true to form, let herself in using her key and appeared in the kitchen expecting tea. It wasn't long before she began her weekly mantra and Jim hated her for it.

'This place is too big for you, Dad,' Penny said. 'You'll be 80 next birthday. Why not consider downsizing? I worry about you, shuffling round in this huge place.'

'I don't shuffle and I manage,' he huffed. 'We've had this conversation before and I'm not ready to move. Biscuit?'

Penny first mentioned the *D* word three years ago, just before Jim's 77th birthday and he'd thought about it every day since. Each time the subject was raised, he was aware of a dense cold spot in the centre of his chest, clinging to the underside of his sternum and wondered if it was fear. He knew she wanted to warehouse him in some dreadful retirement home, had her eyes on his house for a while and if Jim moved out, she could move in – or so she thought – but he wasn't ready. Even if he was, he wouldn't choose to live in a place full of old folk, propped in chairs lining the walls of a ghastly common room, where the television is too loud and the staff call everyone 'love'. Not Jim's idea of the future and he'd been devising a plan to avoid it. Having a plan eased the coldness in his chest.

Penny sipped her tea: 'You *say* that, but you don't manage do you? The garden is too big, you *pay* someone to cut the grass. Think of the money you'll save if you move.'

'It's not about money, I have enough to see me out. Another cup?' he offered.

'You don't use half the rooms and need a cleaner once a month,' she continued. 'If you *downsized* you'd be able to do the housework yourself.' She wiped a finger along the worktop and examined it critically.

'Let's change the subject,' he said. 'I'm happy the way things are and if anything changes, I'll let you know. How's the shop going?'

Penny owned a boutique florist a couple of miles away. The place never made a profit, but she wasn't really committed to the venture, believed that just *owing* a business was what made the money. She'd always been unreliable and eventually the few customers she did have deserted when wreaths and bouquets they'd ordered weren't delivered on time.

'I wanted to talk to you about the business,' she said. 'I have a bit of a cash flow problem and wondered if you'd give me a loan; rent's due at the end of the week and the suppliers have to be paid.'

'Not again,' Jim groaned. 'I can't keep doing this, I'm

not a bottomless pit and you're not good at paying your debts.'

'What?' she exploded. 'I *always* pay you back.'

'You borrowed £500 last month and I haven't seen that yet.'

'But you *will!* Lend me another £500 and I'll pay you the whole lot next month.'

Jim shook his head: 'I'm sorry, I don't have it to lend.'

'Rubbish!' she snapped. 'You're loaded. £500 is nothing to you, but to me it's the difference of running a business or losing it. You *have* to help me.'

'No, I don't. You're a grown woman, Penny, time to stand on your own feet. Doesn't it bother you – fleecing money from an old man?'

She sprang to her feet, eyes angry, skin flushed.

'How dare you say that, how dare you?' She snatched her coat from the back of the chair and stormed out, slamming the front door viciously.

Jim was sorry they'd argued – again – but wasn't sorry she'd gone. He'd never really liked Penny and knew that was a terrible thing to think, but realised it was the truth. Her mother spoiled her right from the off. Penny's birth had been difficult and for a day or two, he thought he'd lose them both. He was so grateful they survived he'd do anything for either of them, but nothing he did for his daughter ever seemed to be good enough. She was a whingy, clingy child who had grown into a sullen, materialistic teenager, who morphed into a materialistic adult.

The chirp of the telephone dragged Jim from his thoughts.

'Hello?'

'Hi, Jim, Colin here. Fancy a swift half at the Beaufort?'

'Definitely! I could do with a beer, Penny's just left in a strop.'

Colin chuckled: 'You'll need something stronger then. I'll see you in half an hour.'

Carrying two pints through the pub lounge, Jim noticed how badly his hands shook. Putting the drinks on the table, he pulled out a handkerchief and wiped his sticky fingers, wondered if the tremor was due to old age, or the coldness in his chest.

Colin raised his glass: 'Cheers.' He slurped his drink. 'So, how is the lovely Penny today?'

'Much the same,' Jim said. 'Still a cow. She's back on the downsizing initiative again, can't wait to pack me off, get her hands on the house and what's left of my savings. I can't believe such a gentle, generous woman like my Gwen, could ever give birth to a child like Penny. Complete opposites.'

'Will you move?' he

'If I do, it won't be into one of those revolting homes, be like prison, *worse*. At least in prison the inmates would be interesting, have some tales to tell, bet they don't sit around all day staring into space.'

'You're probably right, Jim, but I'm not sure care home residents beat each other up or take spice. Another?'

Jim nodded and Colin headed towards the bar, returning with two pints and a couple of whiskey chasers. A bit excessive Jim thought for a lunchtime drink, but drank them anyway and the alcohol encouraged him to talk.

'Penny asked for another loan,' he muttered. 'Over the last few years she's had about twenty grand off me. Turns out not only was I lending her cash, she was helping herself to savings in the building society account. I told Gwen setting up a power of attorney was a bad idea, but she was sure we could trust our own daughter.'

'That's terrible,' Colin said. 'Are you going to do anything about it?'

'Planning to.'

'Will you report her to the police?'

'No, don't think so, I'd like to kill her,' Jim growled. 'How *could* she do such awful things? She stole from Gwen too and I'm partly to blame for the way Penny is, wasn't strict enough, far too lenient. Nasty cow, I could throttle her with my bare hands.'

Colin looked uneasy and Jim laughed to lighten the mood.

'Of course, I'm not *going* to, but I'd like to. One for the road?'

Penny returned two days later. She must really need the money Jim thought, to visit so soon after her tantrum. He made tea and polite conversation, but could tell she wasn't listening.

'Sorry I lost it, Dad, but I'm under a lot of stress,' she said. 'I really *do* need that money and you *will* get it back, I promise.'

'Penny, I told you, I can't give you any more. You've had quite enough over the years and there is no more to give you. Please stop asking because the answer isn't going to change.'

'I'll go bust!'

Jim felt his temper stir and the cold patch in his chest began to heat up rapidly.

'Tough!' he snapped. 'It's about time you started taking responsibility for yourself.'

'I can't believe I'm hearing this,' Penny spluttered. 'Just get your bloody chequebook out.'

'I won't. You've had enough from me – and your poor mother when she was alive. I'm guessing you're only here because you haven't been able to get any money from the cash machine. I've cancelled the card to stop you stealing any more.'

Penny's face reddened: 'I haven't stolen anything!' she screeched.

'And now you're lying to me – again.' He took a deep breath. Words he'd wanted to say for years finally left his mouth. 'Did you really think I wouldn't notice when you stole your mother's jewellery? Hope you got a good price and what did you do with your ill-gotten gains? Clothes, shoes, expensive holidays?'

'I . . . I . . .' Penny stammered.

Jim held his hand up to silence her.

'Whatever you have to say, I'm not interested. You've always stolen from us, remember how I caught you with your fingers in my wallet when you were ten? I should have beaten you then, taught you right from wrong, but your mother wouldn't allow it, said you'd grow out of it. You didn't though.'

He opened a drawer under the counter, slipped out his

father's old service revolver and pointed it at his daughter. Her eyes widened, cheeks flushed crimson and for once she had nothing to say.

'Well, Penny, I've had enough. As you pointed out, I'm nearly eighty and haven't many years left. I shall live what's left of my life knowing that a scheming, money grabbing cow like you isn't in it and don't care if I live those last years in prison.'

He pulled back the hammer, took hold of the stock with both hands and squeezed the trigger.

The judge handed down a life sentence with a tariff of ten years, not bad for attempted murder and brilliant no one suggested Jim was suffering mental incapacity. He'd always been concerned he might end up in Broadmoor, but the plan he'd been concocting for years – ever since Penny first mentioned the *D* word – worked perfectly.

Colin was a marvellous witness and recounted word for word their last meeting, when Jim told him he wanted to kill his daughter. Another customer – ear-wigging on the table next to their's – corroborated the story. Penny told her side of things, leaving out any mention of the money she'd extorted from her father and he didn't mention it either. The gun was obviously Jim's, his fingerprints were all over it.

The media loved the story, reported how lucky it was Jim's tremor caused him to miss. It wasn't luck. He'd aimed to miss. He would never kill his daughter, or anyone come to that. He wasn't a violent man, but was a good shot.

HMP Heatherlea wasn't bad, three meals a day, TV in

the cell and Jim had a bank robber pad-mate. Karl was fascinating, had an unlimited supply of ripping yarns and was good to the elderly man, said he reminded him of his grandfather. He collected Jim's meals, made sure he never had to wait in the post queue and escorted him to and from the association room – lively place with the odd fight – but Jim was never bored or lonely.

Penny didn't visit, not that he was surprised, but knew *she* would be when she discovered Jim had cancelled the power of attorney and left the house to his new bank robber friend, who had a young family, lived in a tatty council flat and wanted to go straight, sure his money would be used more wisely by him than Jim's hellish daughter and could even do some lasting good.

All Jim had to do now was stay in *just* enough trouble with the screws to *lose* remission, but not get shipped out to a different prison. He was settled and didn't relish moving. It was a bit of a juggling act, but he was improving all the time.

DO DRAG QUEENS DO FUNERALS?

I guess I'd always known my father had a second life, a dark secret he kept close to his chest and certainly never confided to his family. When I morphed into an adult, I began to search for signs, clues about his hidden life and eventually reached the conclusion he was in the thrall of, 'the love that dare not speak its name'. Discovering his secret had been a difficult task, Dad had been careful and it wasn't until he reached his eighties I knew for sure – but didn't tell him I'd found out.

The truth didn't shock me, it made me sad for a man who'd lived an utterly conventional life, a good and responsible life, expected by society. He'd never been able to be who he really was. When he died at 83, I was determined to find some way to pay homage to his secret and the opportunity unexpectedly presented itself when Mum asked me to handle the funeral arrangements and bun-fight after the ceremony. It didn't take long to come up with the perfect solution. I would book a drag queen to attend the service – not an outrageous one, a smart, attractive, classy one and it would be *my* secret; my tribute to my father.

I searched online, staggered how many sites advertised drag queens for hire; singing ones, dancing ones, obese ones and ones with full beards – which struck me as a little odd. Each 'girl' had a write-up which listed their individual talents – 'Not an end of the pier girl',

'Dance moves like Madonna', and one that stated, 'Not a dry eye in the house'. I thought I'd hit gold, until I read the ad again. What it actually said was, 'Not a dry *seat* in the house'. I shuddered.

About to give up on my crazy plan, I spotted a website offering, 'Walkabout Queens', and without too much thought, dialled the number on the screen. A husky female voice answered – well, I thought it was female.

'Good morning, Walkabout Queens. You're speaking to Crystal, how may I help you?'

It was patently obvious I hadn't properly prepared for the conversation when the words which left my mouth were: 'Do drag queens do funerals?'

The husky voice chuckled: 'We all do those eventually, sweetheart.'

'No, I mean . . . uh . . . could I hire one to attend a funeral?'

Another throaty chuckle: 'You can hire a queen for just about everything – within reason – we all have limits. What have you in mind?'

'My dad has died, he was 83, and well, I always knew there was *something,* that he had a secret none of us knew,' I gabbled. 'I discovered what it was and thought a drag queen at his funeral would honour his memory. No one else would know, certainly not the family. I just wanted to do something special for him.' My nervous mouth ran away with me, but Crystal remained silent so I continued. 'He'd not been able to live *his* life, the one he would have chosen for himself and I dreamt up this mad idea.' I sighed: 'It's daft, sorry. I shouldn't have bothered you.'

'No, honey, it's fine. You wouldn't *believe* how many funeral gigs we cover and for much the same reasons.'

'You do?' I was surprised.

'More than you'd imagine, and yes, *Walkabout Queens* can help you. We have a lovely girl on our books – Daniella, tall, curvy and beautiful. She's attended funerals before, so if you give me the details, I'll arrange everything.'

Without further thought I provided date, time, location and my credit card details.

A week later family and friends gathered at the pretty church in the village where my father had spent most of his adult life, the village where I was born. There was an exceptional turnout. Dad had been well-respected, a retired engineer, a man with a shed who could fix anything from vacuum cleaners to traction engines and was happy to help out neighbours.

I sat in the front row with mum, the pews behind packed and took a sneaky peek at her face. She seemed calm and relaxed, dry cheeked and gripped my hand tightly as we waited, while sombre organ music swirled around us, air heavy with the scent of lilies and candlewax. There was no sign of Daniella, not that I knew what she looked like, and realised I was glad. On reflection, my great idea probably hadn't been as great as I thought, but just before the service began, I heard the click of the church door and snatched a discrete glance down the aisle. Fascinated, I watched a tall, very black and incredibly beautiful woman float in gracefully and settle on a pew at the back.

Mum dug me in the ribs: 'Stop fidgeting, Linda and face the front,' she hissed. I did as I was told, my head snapped around and faced the front. The service commenced but I couldn't concentrate on the words intoned by the vicar in the slow, drippy voice nearly all vicars use. This was not the way I wanted to remember Dad so tuned out and sank into own thoughts. Somewhere in the middle, my mobile chirped and mum glared at me. I ferretted in my pocket, turned off the device and gave myself a hard time for not remembering earlier.

When all the hymns had been sung and all the prayers said, the assembled congregation, led by the minister, decamped to the graveyard for the burial. I was grateful the sun was shining, there was nothing more depressing than a group of mourners standing around a muddy pit in the rain, watching as a coffin was lowered slowly inside. Daniella stood respectfully by the graveside, head bowed and I was able to take a better look at her.

She was probably early fifties and immaculately turned out. A stylish, black silk dress covered her shapely body, deep purple scarf tied at her throat, which matched a purple, satin band on a wide-brimmed, black hat. Tasteful diamond studs captured the sun's rays, sparkled in her ears and cast minuscule rainbows against her nigrescent skin. She wore patent leather stilettoes, tiny bows on the heels and held a delicate, lace-edged handkerchief in a gloved hand, ready to catch her tears. She was perfect and I wished Dad was here to see her. I nodded in her direction and she smiled at me.

Mum noticed us exchange glances and grabbed my hand: 'Who *is* that?' she whispered.

'Don't know. If she comes to the buffet, I'll try and find out.'

'I've read about funeral gate crashers,' Mum huffed. 'Maybe she's one of those – we don't know any black people.'

I kept my mouth firmly shut. The minister read a psalm – a section of number 103 I think – followed by the ashes to ashes, dust to dust thing and everyone murmured, 'Amen'. An undertaker with a sad, baggy face, offered mourners a handful of dry earth from a wooden box to pitch on top of the coffin. After a respectful pause, the throng began to drift away from the graveside.

We left the burial ground and headed in the direction of the back room at the local pub and Daniella followed the mourners. I was delighted to see she hadn't left after the internment and hoped to snatch a quiet word during the buffet. I supported my mother as we walked the short distance across the village green to the appropriately named, *Engineers' Arms* and once settled inside, a double gin and tonic in her hand, she held court as friends and neighbours sat with her to talk about Dad. At last I was able to sneak away and threaded my way through the crush of well-wishers towards Daniella who was standing alone at the far end of the bar.

I held out my hand in greeting: 'How lovely to see you. Thank you so much for coming.' I leaned in closer. 'You look absolutely fabulous, I couldn't have asked for more. Dad would have been overjoyed.'

She politely took my hand and squeezed my

fingers: 'You must be Linda,' she said. 'Delightful to meet you.' She air-kissed my cheek.

'Yes, that's me.' I said and blushed. 'I'm so glad you could come and pay homage to Dad's secret life. I haven't told anyone else.'

'Very wise,' Daniella said, 'I'm pretty certain your mother wouldn't be pleased.'

'No, you're right, and the reason I've never mentioned it. I'm the only one who knows.'

'How did you find out?'

'Years of clandestine snooping to be honest, it upset me Dad hadn't been able to live the way he wanted.'

'That's often the way,' she said. 'We never really know anyone.' She raised her wine glass: 'To your Dad.'

We clinked and sipped.

'You're very beautiful,' I said, 'and your dress is just gorgeous. Does it take you long to get ready?'

She raised a perfectly sculptured eyebrow: 'No longer than anyone else I would imagine.'

'Of course not, no, I'm sorry, that was inappropriate, but I've never spoken to anyone like you before.'

I received another quizzical look in response: 'Someone like me?' she asked.

I realised I was digging my own hole and two in a single day was excessive, so put down the metaphorical shovel, smiled and tried to conceal my embarrassment.

I clasped her elegant hand: 'Thank you for being here,' I said. 'It's so wonderful to see you and you played your part perfectly. Now, I must mingle or people will wonder. Thank you again.'

I left her at the bar, found an empty seat next to Mum and listened as one of her neighbours spoke in glowing terms about Dad; how kind he was, how helpful, how he'd fixed her hoover so well it nearly pulled the pile off the carpet. When I next looked around the room I noticed Daniella had left. I wanted to giggle and basked in triumph that I had been able to do this remarkable thing for Dad. I wondered if he was looking down – or up – from wherever he was now and approved. Maybe he was laughing for both of us.

After an hour or so spent listening to a multitude of platitudes, I escaped to the ladies, grateful for a moment alone. I checked my makeup in the large mirror, washed my hands, switched on the mobile and opened the text I'd received during the service.

'Dear Ms Roberts, I am very sorry, but Walkabout Queens is unable to fulfil today's contract. Daniella has been unavoidably delayed and, with so little notice, we have found it impossible to arrange a suitable replacement . . .'

BEACH DRAGONS

I've always loved the sound of the sea it's like breathing, especially at night. I often imagined an immense dragon curled on the beach, gusts from its nostrils stirring dry sand as it emptied its lungs.

I listened. The tide was coming in. A wave ran up the incline, giggled through the shingles above the sand and I hoped I'd parked far enough away. The last thing I wanted to do was get up and move the car, but I'd never get to sleep if I didn't. I struggled out of the heap of quilts, flipped up the seat, wriggled behind the wheel, started the car, reversed 20 metres and killed the engine. Silence returned. The dragon was fainter now and I peered through the condensation covered windscreen.

The moon floated out from behind a cloud and lit up the landscape, white sparkles coated wet rocks and shimmered on the surface of the water. I looked through the driver's window and saw other vehicles pulled up on the rough ground. Next to my car was a van which wouldn't look out of place in the Australian outback; camouflage paintwork and a large roof rack with a bicycle and water containers strapped in place. Small porthole-like windows in the roof glowed pale orange and confirmed someone was inside. I envied the van. My old Volvo estate wasn't really a camper but it would have to do.

I crawled into the back, refolded the driver's seat,

fluffed up my nest and snuggled under the mound trying to get warm and comfortable enough to drop off. I hadn't been sleeping well since I started living in the car and it was affecting my work – I was a carer in a residential home. Last week my boss had caught me napping in the staff room and had a right go. I apologised profusely and promised it wouldn't happen again. I couldn't tell her I was homeless and sleeping on the beach – she might have sacked me.

Another reason I couldn't tell her was because I didn't believe it myself. At 62-years-old, I'd worked hard all my life and had precisely *nothing* to show for it, other than the Volvo and a few basic belongings required for survival. I tried to stop my negative thoughts, concentrated on the sound of the waves and hoped they would lull me to sleep.

My ears detected a new sound, a deep menacing growl and I held my breath, then stifled a giggle when I realised the noise was my neighbour snoring. Just to be sure, I peeped through the side window and saw the van's lights were out. I turned over, inadvertently stirred my brain and off it went again and replayed the last few dreadful weeks.

I'd been utterly unprepared for my personal earthquake. The landlord suddenly increased the rent by £200 a month and I was sure I'd be able to manage – I'd always been good at cutting my cloth. I asked for more hours at the nursing home – there weren't any; I advertised for someone to flat share – no one applied. I paid the extra rent for six months and eventually used up my savings, sure I'd find a lodger, or another job – or a miracle. I didn't and needed to move but couldn't find anywhere cheaper, so gave away my stuff, loaded the car with essentials and left the day the rent was due; a moonlight flit. I've felt ashamed and guilty ever since.

A sunbeam brushed my eyelids and woke me with a start. I frantically checked my watch – 6am – and breathed easier, wouldn't be late this morning. I stretched under the covers, delighting in the warmth only ever found in a bed that had been slept in all night. I made sure no one was looking then quickly swapped my night time tee-shirt for my work shirt and added a jumper for warmth. I opened the back door, swung my legs outside and pulled on trousers in one fluid movement, good at incognito dressing. Trainers laced, I grabbed my wash bag, locked the car and dashed to the nearby public toilets, desperate for a pee.

Ten minutes later a tiny stove balanced in the boot and the kettle was on for a morning brew. I shivered. April days can be warm but nights and early mornings were always fresh. I was dreading winter. If I was in the same predicament in a few months, what would November be like? I folded the bedding and tidied the inside of the car while I waited for the water to boil.

The side door of the van opened and a good looking young man jumped down to the compacted shingle. He was tall and lean, middle twenties, athletic build with tanned skin, wearing long baggy shorts, tee-shirt and sandals. He spotted me, smiled and raised a hand and without thinking, I waved back. Why did I do that when I was trying to be invisible?

He wandered over: 'Hi,' he said. 'I'm Fergus.'

'Pat,' I said. 'Short for Patricia, but no one calls me that.' I hesitated then offered him a cuppa. Surprisingly he accepted, went to fetch a mug and returned with two folding chairs he placed in front of the vehicles. We watched the day begin together and shared a packet of biscuits.

'Why are you living on the beach?' Fergus asked.

'Not enough money coming in to pay rent and bills.'

'Haven't been here long have you?'

I shook my head: 'Didn't think I'd be here at all but couldn't find anywhere cheaper or a second job.' I sipped my tea. 'Why do you live in a van?'

'I'm at Medical School, paediatrics. I'm the oldest of eight so pretty good with kids. Got my final exams soon but can't afford tuition fees and rent.'

I chuckled: 'Eight kids is a *huge* family. I'm a singleton, no siblings.'

He grinned over his coffee mug, his eyes danced: 'Strict Catholics my folks, bred like rabbits.'

I checked the time – 6.45am – my shift started at seven and I couldn't be late.

'Will you be here later?' I asked, and didn't really understand why.

'Yeah, should be.'

I packed away the cooker, drove the few miles to work and made it just in time and although my boss frowned, didn't say anything. I wish she'd give me more hours. Sixteen really wasn't enough to keep me going. I couldn't claim a benefit top-up – not having an address any longer – and was too young for a pension. I'd have to do something soon, unconventional living is for the young –

although – a van would be an improvement. Maybe I could save for one.

When my lack of somewhere to live became a reality, I'd contacted the council but they told me they couldn't help as I had, "made myself intentionally homeless" because I'd left the flat before I was evicted. If I'd waited for the bailiffs and endured the horror they would bring with them, I *may* have been offered emergency B & B – on account of my age.

After work I went to the supermarket, bought two gooey cakes and drove back to the beach. As I pulled up, Fergus emerged from his van with two mugs of tea and I presented him with the cakes. The afternoon sun was warm and we sat on the sand chatting. He was great company, witty and intelligent and made me laugh, told silly jokes and stories about other students at school, some of them sounded like fruitcakes. I asked if he had a girlfriend.

He shook his head: 'No, haven't got the time. If I'm not cramming for the finals, I'm pulling pints in the local. I'm hoping that will change when I start work.'

'I'm sure it will,' I said. 'Good looking boy like you should have no trouble.'

He slurped his tea: 'It's not right,' he muttered.

'What isn't?'

'You, having to sleep in a car at your age. Sixth richest country in the world and good people like you are homeless. Haven't you any friends or family you could stay with?'

'No,' I mumbled, embarrassed. 'Dad was my only family, died penniless in a dreadful nursing home and I've

132

always been a bit of a loner. I enjoy my own company.'

That was true until I ended up on the beach, now I wasn't so sure. Perhaps if I'd mixed more with other people someone would have taken me in. I suddenly felt sorry for myself and tried not to cry. If I started I'd never stop and didn't want to drive the young man away.

'Can you play backgammon?' he asked.

'Used to – a long time ago.'

'Marvellous. I haven't played in ages, always a struggle to find anyone who understands the game. Why not come for supper and a game or two? Better than hiding away in your car.'

That was how our friendship began. Nearly every evening I'd go to the van, Fergus and I would share supper then battle each other across the board and we talked; we never stopped talking. My tiny world had suddenly grown. Fergus told me about his gap year – which had morphed into two – and his travels around Asia. He was so funny – I don't think I ever laughed as much in my old life – and I slowly adjusted to sleeping in the car. Going to sleep with the sound of the waves and waking to the call of oyster catchers had a lot going for it. My boss had given me a few more hours, still not enough to rent anywhere, but more money was useful and each week I tried to save the extra to put towards a van of my own.

As summer began the beach grew busier. A council man wandered around every few days and peered suspiciously at the small community of vehicle dwellers, but didn't ask anyone to leave. In July a pair of police officers came knocking and I instantly felt like a criminal, wishing I could melt into the shingle.

Fergus complained bitterly: 'Do you knock on houses with lights on?' he demanded. 'No, of course you don't, so if we're not in contravention of *anything,* why did you disturb us?' The police left us alone after that.

Different vehicles came and went. Some contained people on holiday, but a few were homes. I wondered if anyone was counting the homeless who lived in cars and vans. We didn't fit anywhere; we weren't travellers, or rough sleepers, or sofa surfers. I knew someone counted the others, but was anyone counting us? Did anyone know about us or even care?

The weather turned, a spell of wind and rain blew in and hung around for days. Hunkering down in the car during an endless rain storm wasn't much fun and reminded me I had to sort out something for the winter.

On the day of Fergus' last exam I cooked a celebratory supper on his stove in the van. I'd found some price-reduced steak at the supermarket and cooked it to perfection, served with mashed potato and vegetables. It was the best meal I'd eaten in ages. Fergus brought a bottle of wine from the pub and we toasted his inevitable success, certain he would pass with flying colours. We lounged on the bunk and sipped wine.

'I've something to tell you, Pat,' he said.

'Nothing bad I hope?' I tittered, the wine had softened my brain.

He hesitated and I panicked inside. It *was* something bad, I knew it was.

'What?' I prompted and dreaded the answer.

'I'm going away for a while.'

'How long?' My heart tapped my ribcage in alarm.

'Two weeks if all goes according to plan, but could be longer. I'll be back before the end of August though for definite.'

'August?' I heard a quiver in my voice and hoped Fergus hadn't noticed. 'Where are you going?'

'I have a job offer in the Midlands – dependent on my results. They want me to go for an interview and assessment and I'll need to find somewhere to live. Might as well get everything done at once, rather than travel back and forth.'

I tried to sound pleased for him, delighted even, but wasn't fooling anyone. What would I do without him living next door and *why* had I allowed myself to get so attached and dependent?

'You'll be alright won't you?' he asked.

'Of course,' I lied. 'I'll be fine, don't worry. I *will* miss you though – and the backgammon.'

'Me too . . . but I'll be back, tell you where I'll be living, just in case you ever take to the road.'

In the morning he'd gone and I cried, couldn't help myself. I rested my cheek on the window and tears mingled with running condensation on the glass. I couldn't stop and cried for the last few months of awfulness, for the loss of my new friend, for the loss of hope. I wasn't sure I could stay here without Fergus, didn't know any of the other van dwellers and didn't want to. They weren't very friendly.

I couldn't face work so called my boss, told her I was

ill and should be in tomorrow. As usual she didn't make the conversation easy but grudgingly agreed to my absence. I spent most of the day in bed, unable to face a day without conversation or friendship and the prospect of having to spend future evenings in the car. I'd always felt safer in the van and ached for Fergus, a deep physical pain as though I'd suffered a bereavement.

When I finally summed up enough enthusiasm haul myself out of bed, I dressed, put the kettle on and while I waited for it to boil, walked up and down the dry patch of stone where the van had been parked, feeling utterly desolate.

Two weeks later when the rain finally blew away I had a day off. I tidied my home, then locked the doors and set off to walk the length of the beach. In the old days when I needed to keep busy I'd clean, but there wasn't much to do in the Volvo, so I'd discovered long tramps along the sand were a good distraction. They helped a little, brought me some fleeting peace, but all I wished for was to know how Fergus was and if I would ever see him again.

During one of my walks I met a woman with a hairy, bouncy dog that was tearing up and down the beach, barking madly and chasing seagulls.

The woman walked towards me: 'Sorry to disturb your peace,' she said. 'Toby's been coped up all day so he's letting off steam.'

'Yes, isn't he,' I agreed. 'Cute little chap.'

The woman slipped into step beside me and we walked together. She was smartly dressed, hair nicely done, clanking jewellery on one wrist and a lovely pair of shoes –

not really suited for the beach. Younger than me, 35 maybe?

'Are you on holiday?' I asked.

'No, I live here, lovely spot apart from the bloody gypos who've set up near the beach. You must have seen them. I've rung the council several times but they're useless, don't know *why* I pay my council tax. Do you know they use the beach as a toilet? Disgusting.'

I was shocked by her response and didn't know whether to admit I was one of the "gypos" or not and decided not, but wanted to tell her she was being unfair.

'They don't have anywhere else to go,' I said gently. 'Many have jobs but don't earn enough to pay rent so live in their vehicles . . . and they use the public toilets.'

'Bloody eyesore,' the woman grumbled. '"Uninterrupted view of the sea" the estate agent said and he was right, until this bunch of losers moved in. Won't do anything for house prices.'

I couldn't stand her sanctimonious attitude any longer.

'Lady,' I said, 'you're lucky to *have* a house, the people on the beach haven't. They're not here by choice.'

'Of *course* they are,' she sneered. 'Junkies and alcoholics getting bombed all day. They should get a job.'

I glared at her: 'I've got a job!' I yelled and stormed back to the car.

It began to rain so I dived inside and wept. I seemed to be doing a lot of that since Fergus left. It was as though I'd been abandoned. The pain in my chest was unbearable and I wondered if I had a crush on him – at my age. Maybe it was because I *knew* he wouldn't be coming back.

Why would he bother? His life wasn't on the beach.

I pulled myself together, changed into dry clothes and made sandwiches for supper – easier than cooking in the car. After the rain, a gale blasted the shoreline. The breathing on the beach was louder as though the dragon was angry and sand grains picked up by the wind chinkled and hissed against the windows. I curled in my nest with a novel from Oxfam. The tagline said, "the funniest thing since Bridget Jones", but I didn't laugh once, so packed it in, pulled the quilts over my head and gave up on the day.

In the morning the sun had returned, the dragon was sleeping and Fergus was back! His van was the first thing I saw when I wiped the window and felt such joy. I opened my door quietly and padded silently around the camper. I heard him snoring and knew I'd have to wait for him to wake up, so rang in sick – again – then dashed to the local shop and bought the makings of breakfast.

When I returned Fergus was sprawled on a chair sipping coffee. He smiled broadly and hauled himself upright.

'Pat! Where were you? I was worried.'

I waved the bag: 'Buying breakfast. Haven't had a fry-up since you left. Can I use your cooker?'

'Help yourself, a fry-up sounds marvellous.'

He followed me inside the van and I noticed how clean and tidy it was.

'Have you decorated?' I asked.

'Yeah, a bit,' he said and flopped on the bunk, 'but never mind that, how have things been with you?'

'Much the same. The only highlights were a slanging match with a resident – I objected to being labelled as a junkie-gypo-scrounger – and the car needed a new tyre. How about you?'

'Got the job I went for, junior doctor in a paediatrics department and even found a flat share I can afford. Things are good.'

'That's wonderful. I'm really proud of you.'

I dished out sausages and bacon, fried bread and scrambled egg and Fergus tucked in as though he hadn't eaten since he'd left. The meal finished we slumped on the wide bunk, too full to speak and enjoyed the togetherness. The beach was quiet, other vehicle dwellers were parked further away and being mid-week there were fewer day-trippers. I thought I saw the dog woman and wondered if she'd spotted me, but didn't care; not today.

'How are you getting on looking for a place?' Fergus asked.

'Rubbish. There's nothing about and the council are adamant I don't fit into the right box to be housed, so I'm buying long johns ready for winter.' I put the kettle on to wash up. 'I'm saving for a van though, boss gave me a few more hours.'

'No work today?'

'Day off,' I lied.

'I wondered,' he said, 'whether you'd do me a favour.'

'I can't imagine what I could possibly do for you, but of course – if I can. What is it?'

'My job is in the centre of Birmingham and be to honest, parking the van in the staff car park will be a nightmare, people are bound to complain. I don't need

139

Bessie – the van that is – as I have a flat, so I'm planning to get a car instead.'

'That makes sense,' I said, realising sadly he wouldn't come to camp on the beach.

'Well . . .' he hesitated. 'I wondered if we could do a swap.'

'A what?'

'A swap. You let me have your car and you can have the van.' He smiled at me, eyes full of light and excitement.

'I . . . I don't know what to say,' I stammered. 'It's an amazingly kind offer, but I can't let you give me your van.'

'I'm not giving it, I'm swapping it and of *course* you can.'

During the remainder of the daylight, we moved our belongings and as Fergus emptied drawers and cupboards, I emptied cardboard boxes and arranged my clothes properly for the first time since I left the flat. We chatted non-stop, ate supper and played backgammon. When it was time for him to leave I patted my old car, he told Bessie to take good care of me, we hugged and promised to keep in touch. I watched him pull away, happy in the knowledge we would meet again, then climbed in the van, locked the doors and closed the curtains.

Soft lighting lit the interior and a night heater warmed the air, it was cosy, private – perfect. Stretched out in bed, I glanced up at the tiny porthole windows and saw the stars, listened to the breathing dragon, the giggle of waves on shingle and knew I'd experienced a miracle.

140

THE GAME CHANGER

Jack burrowed deeper inside the bramble thicket beneath the trees of Hangman's Copse, wondered why he had ever thought this was a good idea and why he'd come alone. What a numbskull. He knew people who would have been happy to accompany him, so why hadn't he asked someone? Maybe more than one. There was that saying about safety in numbers. Well, *they* had the numbers and Jack didn't feel safe.

He peered through the mass of tangled briars, winced as a thorn snagged his thigh and concentrated on the sounds of the wood. The day was mild, damp and still. No breeze ruffled the late autumn foliage or stirred the air. Jack listened to a flock of redwings working through the wood as they foraged for berries; the jarring call of a startled pheasant like a football rattle with a stammer; an unkindness of ravens high in the treetops that croaked and honked at each other, and in the distance Jack heard *them.* Their shouts and discordant whoops echoed across the stillness of the open fields, dogs barked and Jack became aware of a vibration in his chest caused by the pounding of hooves drawing closer. He shuddered. They mustn't find him. Why had he chosen to come alone? Stupid, brainless idiot!

He shifted position and knelt on wet ground, a cold dampness seeped through his trousers and another bramble clawed viciously at the back of his hand and drew blood. He sucked the line of crimson beads. He knew he should call for help, make a run for it . . . something, but his fear was accompanied by a kind of paralysis and he remained where he was, frozen in terror to the saturated earth.

He'd left everything too late, he knew that now. What was the point of being a hero if he was a dead hero? All his life he'd been cautious, afraid to step out of the box he'd been assigned at birth and the only time he'd been brave enough to take a risk, this happened. He had to admit, he didn't feel like a hero, he was scared witless.

He prayed his pursuers rode on past, that they hadn't spotted him taking cover in the copse. They were closer now, louder and Jack could make out snatches of conversation.

'This way, he . . .'

'I saw him . . .copse . . .'

'Here . . .in the trees!'

Jack began to tremble when he heard them crash into the undergrowth. Horses whinnied, a whip cracked, the dog pack began to bay and through the cacophony, sliced the scream of a bird of prey, no doubt balanced on the forearm of one of the riders.

Jack swallowed a whimper and realised – again too late – he hadn't properly thought things through. What would happen if he was discovered? What would they do? Beat him? Hurt him? *Kill* him? He gave himself a mental shake, he was overreacting. No one would die. He concentrated on controlling his breathing, willed his heart to slow and nearly achieved both before his hiding place was unearthed.

A busy rustle announced the arrival of a small brown terrier that slipped easily between thick spiky stems, nose to the ground, energetic tail a blur of motion. For a couple a seconds Jack thought he'd got away with it, then the dog looked up, blinked once and let loose a piercing volley of yaps that alerted its handlers. They followed the sound and soon spotted Jack crouched in his thorny sanctuary.

A large, unkempt looking man with a generous belly, thick forearms and wild hair, ploughed into the middle of the bramble patch, grabbed the shoulder of Jack's coat and hauled him into the open. Jack tried to resist and struggled frantically, but it was useless. He was no match for his captor who flung him on the potholed track in disgust.

'Look what we have here, Master,' the man said, nudging Jack with a heavy boot.

A hook nosed man with pale skin and dark hair sat astride a large bay horse, a Harris hawk perched on his leather clad forearm. He peered down at the fallen man and urged his mount forward as though to trample him. Jack scrabbled through the mud trying to create some distance between his head and the wildly stamping hooves, like a crab racing for retreating waves on an estuary's silted shore. The band of watching horsemen cackled nastily.

'Don't let him escape,' the Master warned. 'I want to hear what he has to say for himself.'

The large man pulled Jack to his feet, he dangled helplessly in the firm grip and wished he was anywhere but here. Other riders had joined the Master and dogs swarmed around the horses' legs, tails held high, eyeing Jack as though he was their next meal.

'Who the hell are you?' the Master growled. 'You're on private property.'

Jack shrugged. He didn't want to answer any questions and knew whatever he said would probably get him in worse trouble, so remained silent, even when his tormentor shook him roughly.

'Answer the Master, you pathetic worm.'

'Haven't got anything to say,' Jack mumbled. 'I don't have to talk to you, any of you. This isn't right.'

'What isn't?' the Master asked. 'Last time I checked, we are completely within our rights to be here. It's *you* who haven't got any rights, *you* who is somewhere he shouldn't be. Well, I'm not having it. I'm going to make an example of you to deter any others from considering this stupid game. Bring him, lads.'

The rider turned his horse and set off along the track followed by the rest of the company and their hounds. Jack was herded in front of two burly men with terriers at their feet. One man poked him painfully with a stick. Jack glanced left and right in panic but couldn't see a way out of the dreadful situation he was in, fearful of what might happen next.

The Master didn't travel far into the wood before he reined his horse in at the base of a large, ancient oak tree.

Jack finally found his voice: 'W. . . what are you going to do with me?'

The Master dismounted and spooked the hawk into another screaming session. The creature spread its wings, flapped madly and russet-red feathers glowed in the morning sunshine like burnished copper. He tied the bird to his saddle, stood in front of the tree and shouted: 'Has anyone got a rope?'

Jack wasn't sure he'd heard properly. A rope? What did the man want a rope for? Were they going to tie him up? Why would they do that?

A younger rider threw a coiled length of thick cord that the Master caught, unrolled, tossed one end over a low sturdy branch and began fiddling with the other.

Jack watched in horror as the man fashioned a slip noose: 'You can't hang me!' he spluttered. 'There are laws.'

'Yes, there are,' the Master sneered and yanked on the noose to check it ran smoothly, 'but they don't apply to us. Never have.'

'If you kill me that will be murder,' Jack said. '*Those* laws apply to you. They apply to everyone.'

The Master laughed: 'Suicide is a different matter though, isn't it? Good spot for it, Hangman's Copse. You aren't the first to die here and you probably won't be the last.'

The guards heaved Jack nearer to the tree and he tried to resist using every spark of life in his soul, but wasn't strong enough. This was *so* wrong. He couldn't believe he was going to die. He had been trying to do the right thing and was now in so much trouble, serious trouble, he doubted he'd ever leave this place. He glanced over his shoulder at his tormentors, trying to catch someone's eye, plead for mercy, but found no sympathy. All he saw was bloodlust, a wild excitement bubbling in each one as they prepared to watch him hang, feet frantically kicking open air.

146

The Master waved the noose and Jack dug his heels into the soft loam with little effect. The Harris hawk gripped the pommel of the saddle with acid-yellow talons tipped by long obsidian claws and regarded him coldly. Jack looked deep into its dark eyes and wondered at its beauty, its wildness, as much a prisoner as he was.

'This is bloody daft,' Jack said. 'You won't get away with this.'

'You think,' the Master sneered. 'I am sick to death with the likes of you rampaging through the countryside as though you own it, going wherever you wish as though it's your *right*. I've told you, you have no rights.

His captors dragged him closer and the noose was slipped over Jack's head. The rough barbs of the rope prickled his skin and he thrashed his upper body desperate to escape, but only succeeded in pulling the knot tighter. He tried to swallow and desperately gulped for air as his airway was restricted. He felt woozy, his legs threatened to fail him and then thankfully, he blacked out.

Jack regained consciousness sprawled in the dirt. He cautiously cracked open his eyelids. The clearing was quiet now and deserted; no dogs, no horsemen and no Master. Even the rope was gone and he briefly wondered if he'd dreamt the whole thing.

He swallowed and a hot soreness in his throat informed him it hadn't been a dream. He rolled over and knelt in the sticky mud, sucked in air, rubbed the rope burns on his neck and stared at the churned up ground. He groaned, turned his head slowly towards the heavens

147

and grinned insanely, ecstatic to still be alive.

He hauled himself upright and carefully tested his balance then shuffled a few paces to another dense bramble patch close to the foot of the oak. Rummaging amongst the autumn red leaves, he removed a small device; a mobile phone on a selfie stick. He was delighted with the footage and trembled as he watched his own mock hanging, recognised his absolute terror; he'd been so sure he was going to die.

He tapped the screen with unreliable fingers and after a few unsuccessful attempts called up his substantial and wide ranging mailing list and managed to compose a short covering email:

Attached: Proof of local foxhunt's illegal cubbing expedition. The Master even brought his hawk as cover; as if a Harris could take a fox! Now we have them!

DANCING RATS AND TREBLE CLEFS

(an article)

My writing days are never the same. Some are good, some bad, some *atrocious*. A few are OK – just about – but no two are ever the same.

I'm incredibly blessed. I live in the perfect place for a writer, a small hamlet on a mountain, ten miles away from everything and anything. The spaghetti-tangle of lanes leading to this out-of-the-way place are nearly deserted, consequently traffic noise doesn't disturb me, and as the settlement was built on the edge of a military no-fly zone, there are no noisy aircraft either. True, when the firing ranges are in use the rattle of gunfire percolates my thoughts, but after 12 years of living here, I have become desensitized to the occasional mini battle.

A good friend visiting for the first time proclaimed, "It's all a bit too *'Wicker man'* for me," followed by, "how do you stand it?" That's easy, I love the isolation, the absence of people, the clean mountain air and the peace and quiet.

Today is an excellent writing day, all contact with the outside world has been severed; again. A winter storm is sweeping across the high tops. Monsoon-like rain splats on the window above my desk, as wind screams over the village squatting on the mountain. The gale has torn down power lines and toppled mobile phone masts. Ironically, the water has also been cut off. I'd kill for a cuppa. A steaming cup of strong coffee should always be within reach while I'm writing. Coffee is the only missing element today, everything else is perfect thanks to the angry weather.

I've covered my desk with *proper* paper, smooth and heavy – I detest writing on rubbishy paper – and my elderly fountain pen is filled with the beautiful purple ink I love. I've now spent nearly an hour covering an entire page with doodles and large clusters of treble clefs. These musical symbols are particularly pleasing to craft using a nib that strokes the paper. Ball points skid across surfaces like ice skaters, scratching groves. Despite my careful preparations – as yet – on this perfect writing day, nothing worthwhile has materialised on my expensive sheet of A4.

The storm snatches away my attention. I gaze out of the window and watch as garden birds battle the roaring wind. Things are quieter inside the house, the sounds smaller, but no less intrusive. Rainwater drips down the chimneys and sizzles on hot wood burners – the burnt-tar smell isn't remotely pleasant – and I'm aware of a rat in the cavity walls; sounds as though it's dancing the cha-cha. Rustle, scrabble, squeak-squeak. Rustle, scrabble, squeak-squeak.

There are always distractions and if *they* don't stop me writing, there are the excuses. I should be hoovering, dusting, hauling fire-wood inside, and the ironing pile is growing to ridiculous proportions. Excuses are easier to ignore when the power is out, making some tasks impossible, but they continue to stalk me and hiss in my ear.

151

My undisciplined thoughts drift towards summer. On warm days, I camp out on what I laughingly refer to as my "*Sun Terrace*", a small area of pretty gravel at the back of the house, a natural sunshine trap. I have a comfortable seat which began life in the front of a transit van and a large empty cable-spool from a DIY store serves as a side table; somewhere to plonk the essential coffee mug.

Outdoor writing is the best! I'm convinced warmth from the sun charges up my internal batteries and jump starts my brain and empty pages are covered with purple at a fantastic rate. The writing isn't always good, but always worthwhile and always enjoyable, a meditation of sorts. Empty your mind, ignore external distractions, refill your mind with words that knit into sentences and construct prose. It's the closest thing to magic I know.

But today – this *excellent* writing day – the army of treble clefs has triumphed and marches across the page in platoons.

My mind wanders . . . again.

I'm lucky, I have friends who encourage my writing habit. I churn out a regular supply of short stories and they queue up to read them – flattering – but they have little understanding of the work involved. The first week spent thinking as I wander the forests close to home. Writing the first draft – scribbled down over a couple of days, followed by editing, re-writing and more editing that can take at least a week. Next, ignore the new creation for another week before reading it to the dogs and editing some more.

So, why do I pick up my pen every day? Because the thrill of finishing a piece of work, reading it out loud and hearing the words dance in the air is my reward, the rush I crave. I don't conjure magic every day, far from it, but there is always the chance that it *will* happen, the hope that something special will appear. Curiously, I've discovered that if I don't use my Waterman every day, I suffer withdrawal symptoms – does that make me a junkie?

Electricity still hasn't been restored. I watch the storm safely from behind the glass and spare a thought for the crews of engineers climbing poles, praying they held on tight as they battled with the gale.

A sparrow hawk zips past my window, chasing a blue tit supper and I realise I've been distracted yet again. I glare at the miniature graffiti marring the surface of good paper and growl audibly. I'm sure a hot drink would lubricate my brain. I make do with a glass of cold milk, re-fill my pen, slip another blank sheet of paper from the pile and light candles.

The golden glow shrinks my study and as dusk ends and night begins, the window glass turns black and outside disappears. Everything is quieter now. The rats in the walls appear to be sleeping and the storm has spun away from my mountain to torment someone else.

The blank page accuses me, proves that I'm a hopeless scatterbrain. I've been crouching over my desk for hours and haven't produced anything worthwhile. My eyes are drawn to a rejection letter pinned on the notice board. I kept this one to remind myself how dismissive – and, whisper it, rude – some literary agents can be and as I stretch up to rip it down, the magic arrives. A stray gust of wind funnels down the chimney, a title floats onto the page and words begin to stream from my pen.

Sometime later, electricity is suddenly restored and the room fills with bleeps and chirps as devices power up and the overhead light makes me blink. The abrupt change is unwelcome. I slap off the lights, preferring the yellow candlelight, and continue writing. As the evening slips away, the paper fills and hours later I realise I'm thirsty and it's way past bedtime. I make the long overdue coffee and carry the mug carefully up to my bedroom. I slip under the duvet, sip strong coffee and read what I've written.

The title is *great* . . .

Acknowledgements

With thanks to the members of the Writers' Circle for their encouragement and advice and my 'reading panel' for their tireless work, Bill, Erica, Helen, Kerry, Pauline and Saturday Sue. Thanks also to Peter, for his valuable IT knowledge which made this book possible. And lastly – thanks to the Tattooed Man.

About the author

Nicola began keeping a journal after receiving a five year diary on her sixth birthday from her grandmother.

Her work has been published in *The Interpreter's House* journal, and *Scribble Magazine*. She has won several international prizes including the 2017 Wells Festival of Literature Short Story award, and one of her novels was shortlisted at Hastings Lit Fest 2018.

She has worked as a banker, jeweller, model engineer, bouncer and prison visitor, and currently lives on a remote Welsh mountain with a dog and fountain pen for company.

Printed in Great Britain
by Amazon